I WISH I COULD SAY THAT F... pinched and I wondered if I should really be doing this. I definitely wish I'd given God, the Flagpole Girls, and even my "family" a second thought.

But I'm not sure I did. I only know I gazed at those beads thinking one thing: *Fletcher likes purple.*

I had to have them.

And I did. They were in my hand, suddenly dull against the sparkles of sweat in my palm. I think I really did get a pinch in my chest then, a knot that made me whisper to myself, *Wait a minute.*

I closed my fingers over the beads. Then I opened them. My hand moved back to the bins they had come from—and then I pulled my hand toward my pocket.

The door jangled and a springy voice said, "How did it go?"

It was Angel Lady. I convulsed like I was having a seizure. Beads went everywhere.

Dear Parent,

Thank you for considering Nancy Rue's book for your teen. We are pleased to publish her *Raise the Flag* series and believe these books are different than most you will find for teens.

Tragically, some of the things our teens face today are not easy to discuss. Nancy has created stories and characters that depict real kids, facing real-life issues with real faith. Our desire is to help you equip your children to act in a God-pleasing way no matter what they face.

Nancy has beautifully woven scriptural truth and direction into the choices and actions of her characters. She has worked hard to depict the issues in a sensitive way. However, I would recommend that you scan the book to determine if the subject matter is appropriate for your teen.

Sincerely,

Dan Rich
Publisher

Raise the Flag Series BOOK 3

I ONLY BINGE
ON HOLY HUNGERS

Nancy Rue

WATERBROOK
PRESS
COLORADO SPRINGS

I ONLY BINGE ON HOLY HUNGERS
PUBLISHED BY WATERBROOK PRESS
5446 North Academy Boulevard, Suite 200
Colorado Springs, Colorado 80918
A division of Bantam Doubleday Dell Publishing Group, Inc.

The characters and events in this book are fictional,
and any resemblance to actual persons or events is coincidental.

Unless otherwise noted, scriptures for the Raise the Flag series
are taken from *The Holy Bible, New International Version* (NIV)
© 1973, 1978, 1984 by International Bible Society,
used by permission of Zondervan Publishing House.

ISBN 1-57856-034-9

Published in association with the literary agency of
Alive Communications, Inc., 1465 Kelly Johnson Blvd.
Suite 320, Colorado Springs, Colorado 80920.

Printed in the United States of America
1998—First Edition

10 9 8 7 6 5 4 3 2 1

To my niece Kristen,
who never lets a holy hunger go unfilled

"ARE YOU GOING TO EAT YOUR CRUSTS, TOBE?" I SAID.

Tobey looked from me to the three pieces of pizza crust on her plate and curled her lip. "No," she said. "But you don't want them, do you—after I've been gnawing on them?"

Across the table, Norie snorted. She wasn't being a pig; she always did that. "Of course she wants them. The kid's a garbage disposal. Look out, she'll start nibbling your napkin next."

"I don't do napkins," I said. I eyed the crusts again, and Tobey pushed her plate toward me.

"Cheyenne, don't you like the part with the sauce and cheese?" Shannon said.

I could hardly hear her it was so noisy in Round Table. Plus Shannon talked like a little rabbit. The first two weeks I knew her I thought she had laryngitis all the time. I'm not too quick about stuff like that.

The noise gave me a good excuse to pretend I didn't hear her and just to stuff half a crust in my mouth. The truth was I loved pizza, all of it. I'm one of the few people I know who doesn't barf when somebody orders it with anchovies. But since I didn't help pay for it, I didn't feel like I could take anything but the leftovers.

"Okay, Marissa," Tobey said, "what do we have so far?"

We all chewed in the direction of Marissa Martinez, who

was picking off pepperoni and taking notes at the same time. I think that's why she was always the secretary when we Flagpole Girls got together—because she could write everything down without getting tomato sauce on the paper. That was part of the reason they never asked me to do it. That and because I couldn't spell worth beans, being dyslexic and all.

But don't let me get off the subject. I tend to do that. Norie always said it was because I was a freshman. I don't know; I'd been doing it ever since I could remember.

"Okay," Marissa said, consulting her notes. "We're going to stuff her locker with balloons before school. I can get her combination from the office."

"What would we do if you didn't work in there?" Tobey said.

"Would we have to break in or what?" I said.

Norie rolled her eyes at me and motioned for Marissa to continue. I didn't mind. If Norie stopped rolling her eyes at me, I'd know she didn't love me anymore.

"We grab her right after third period and sing 'Happy Birthday' to her in the locker hall," Marissa went on.

"She's going to be so embarrassed," Shannon said. Her pale blue eyes got big. "You guys aren't going to do that to me on *my* birthday, are you? I'd die."

"No," Norie said, "because I think you would."

Shannon would. She was, like, *way* timid. Which was probably why she had never gotten into half the trouble I had. Matter of fact, as many problems as Tobey and Norie had had in the fall, what with Tobey bringing that sexual assault charge and Norie being accused of cheating, none of them had the record I did. Which was why I was so jazzed to hang out with them. I mean, dude . . .

Well, back to the story.

"Then we get Ira to bring her to the theater lobby at lunch," Marissa was saying.

"Blindfolded," Tobey put in. "We don't want her to see the cake at first."

Marissa scowled at her notes. "Cake?" she said. "Where are we getting a cake?"

Norie narrowed her sharp little eyes at Marissa. "Didn't we decide that?" You had to know Norie or you would think she was ticked off all the time. At first, when we had all met that day for See You at the Pole and none of us knew each other, I thought she hated my guts. Turned out she about saved my life, I mean, not like from dying, just from being sent back to . . .

Okay, back on track. Everybody was looking at each other.

"You're a good cook, Shannon," Tobey said.

But Shannon shook her head so that all that silky blond hair spilled over her eyes. She was so feminine. I wished I were. I had a body like a twelve-year-old boy. Anyway, Shannon's face turned blotchy pink. "I do cookies," she said. "That's it."

"I can make nachos, enchiladas, you name it in the dinner department," Marissa said. "But my cakes always turn out gross."

"What's the big deal?" Norie said. "Can't you just read the package and do it?"

Tobey poked her. Tobey's fudge-brown eyes were doing that dance they did when she was getting ready to tease somebody. "Can't *you?*" she said.

Norie snorted again. "Are you new?" she said. "Have you ever tasted anything I've baked?"

"No," Tobey said.

"There's a good reason for that," Norie said. "They call it ptomaine poisoning. I'm writing the 'This Is Your Life, Brianna Estes' thing. That's my contribution."

Everybody frowned for a second. I occupied myself with the last piece of crust. Just about everyone had made a contribution to Brianna's birthday bash except me. It wasn't that

I wasn't generous. I mean, if I'd had the money, I'd have sprung for the whole thing. But that was just it. Why do you think I was eating the edges of the pizza and hoping Tobey would offer me a sip of her Coke? I'd told them I didn't have any money *with* me. I didn't add that I didn't have any at home either.

But then I had an idea, and before it even finished unfolding itself in my head, I opened my mouth. I did that a lot.

"Tassie can make the cake," I said. "She makes great ones. You should have seen the one she did for Avery's birthday. She put a skateboarder on it and everything."

"Right on, Chey," Norie said. "Tassie's an incredible cook." She grunted. "My mother's idea of getting dinner started is to call Famous Murphy's and talk to the caterer."

"Your mom cooks like that, but you never gain a pound, Cheyenne?" Tobey said. "That's disgusting."

"You should talk," I said. "You're *all* thin!"

"Have you had your eyes checked lately?" Norie said.

Norie wasn't fat. She wasn't all muscly-athletic like Tobey or willowy stick-woman like Shannon and Marissa. She didn't exactly weigh ninety pounds like me, either. But now that she was starting to wear different clothes from those bag lady things she used to put on, you could tell she had a waistline and great legs. She used to wear her coffee-colored hair really short, too, but now she was letting it grow, and I thought she was kind of cute . . .

Now where was I going with all that? Oh, yeah, all the girls were beautiful.

Tobey had strawberry-blond hair that was always kind of fluffy around her face, and her skin was like, shiny.

Marissa was Hispanic, and she was so pretty she made me wish I came from Mexico, too. Or Venezuela. It was one of those places. Anyway, she wore her hair kind of chopped off at the chin, and it was adorable. I'd actually picked up the scissors once to do that to my hair, which is dark and straight and straggles to my shoulders, but Ellie—one of my foster sisters—caught me and said I'd look like an orphan boy if I did that.

Then there was Shannon, so frail looking and delicate, and Brianna, who was her total opposite. She was African-American, and she wore her hair practically shaved. You could tell from her intense, black eyes that she didn't take anything off of anybody.

To tell you the truth, I could never figure out why they kept me around. I wasn't drop-dead gorgeous like all of them, although Marissa was always telling me a lot of girls would give their whole Gap collection to have full lips like mine. I thought they made me look like Mick Jagger, myself.

I couldn't afford to dress like they did. They were Meadowood Mall. I was Kmart, about once a year. They were Rogers' Jewelers; I was earrings and necklaces I made myself.

They all came from these nice, two-parent families. I was in my fourth foster home, not counting that group home in Winnemucca and the time I did at Wittenberg. I loved Tassie, my current foster mom, and Avery, Brendan, Ellie, Felise, and Diesel were getting to be like a family to me. But it wasn't like Tobey with her mom and dad, who was a preacher, and her brother Fletcher, who was a babe . . .

The point is I wasn't anything like any of them. I was the only freshman, even. I was pretty sure they kept me around just because they were such good Christians, and it would have been this major sin to ignore me. I was trying to be like them. They had already taught me a lot about praying, going to God when you're in trouble, having decent people as your friends instead of scum bags like I used to hang out with in Lovelock, and before that Pahrump . . .

But at times like this I felt like a big toe trying to pass as a finger, you know what I'm saying? And it got worse, like in the next second.

"When do we give Brianna her presents?" Shannon said.

"Did you already get her something?" Tobey said.

"Of course she did," Norie said. "She does her term papers the first week of the semester, remember?"

"I couldn't wait," Shannon's eyes turned sparkly. That didn't happen often. Shannon looked kind of sad to me most of the time.

"What did you get her?" Marissa said.

"Watercolors," Shannon said. "They had them on sale at Oakman's. They're in this really neat case."

"Cool," Norie said. "I'm going to buy her some kind of rad sketchbook then. Did anybody else do that?"

Marissa shook her head. "I got her a—"

I didn't hear the rest. I was groaning too loud inside my head. A present? I thought I'd done my thing with the cake. What was I going to use to buy Brianna a present? I'd spent every dime I had on Christmas presents, and this was only January. I hadn't had time to even think about where I was going to get more money.

But I had to buy Brianna a present. She was awesome. She was always setting me straight on stuff and telling me when would be a good time to shut up—that was one of my major things—and making sure I didn't mess up.

Besides, everybody else was buying her something, something totally cool. If I gave her a lame card I drew on construction paper, I was going to look like the kindergartner crashing the big kids' party. My chest started to pinch. It always did that when I was stressed.

"Anybody want the rest of my Coke?" Tobey said.

I came to and snatched it up, nodding even as the glass went to my lips.

"I think she wants it," Norie said in that dry way she has.

"I still have to go shopping for a present," Tobey said.

"What are you getting her?" Shannon said.

"I don't know. It has to be something really different, you know? Brianna's just not ordinary. I'll know it when I see it. Anybody know any bizarre shops in Reno?"

"Ask Ms. Race," Norie said. "She does bizarre."

"She does cool!" I said. Ms. Race was like our adviser, even though we weren't an official club. She was Mr. Holden's, the principal's, secretary, and I'm not sure how she ended up being part of our group. But it was a good thing she was because she seemed to know what to do when the rest of us got stuck.

Maybe I should ask her, I thought. *I mean, you talk about stuck—I am.*

But unless Ms. Race was going to lend me money, I didn't see what good it was going to do. And I never borrowed money. How was I supposed to pay it back? Rob a bank? I might as well rob it in the first place.

But I shook off that thought before it had a chance to grow any bigger. I'd done some—what did they call it—"petty theft" when I was about ten. Between that and my little stay at Wittenberg, I'd had enough run-ins with the law. In fact, one more mess-up, and I was out of Tassie's and back in that Hades-hole.

I know "Hades-hole" sounds lame, but Tassie didn't let us swear. I mostly did what Tassie said. She was the best thing that had ever happened to me. Next to the Flagpole Girls. And God. I started to pray right then: *God, let something happen so I'll have the money.*

"Earth to Cheyenne," somebody said.

I blinked and saw Tobey snapping her fingers in front of my face.

"What?" I said.

"Do you want a ride home?" she said.

Marissa gave her soft little laugh. "Where were you, Cheyenne?" she said.

"Wherever it was, let's not go there," Norie said, giving me one of her you-know-I'm-just-kidding pokes in the rib. "I don't have two hours."

It wouldn't take two hours to tell what I was thinking, I told myself miserably. *"I'm broke" would just about do it.*

But I didn't say it. Instead, I thrashed around in my brain the way I'd rummage through my gym locker, trying to find a way to be like these girls I looked up to.

It was the first mistake in a long line of them.

A long, long line.

CHAPTER ONE

AS WE HEADED ACROSS THE PARKING LOT TO TOBEY'S red Honda, which she called Lazarus because she said it had been brought back from the dead so many times, I tried to concentrate on not falling on my face on the patches of ice. Sometimes it was hard for me to think about more than one thing at a time, and just then buying a present for Brianna was shouting everything else down.

Until Tobey said, "We have to pick up Fletcher at King first. Do you mind?"

Did I mind? Would I mind having Ed McMahon come to the door with the Publisher's Clearinghouse Sweepstakes? Would I mind if Brad Pitt dropped by? Would I mind . . .

Well, you get my drift. Her brother, Fletcher L'Orange, was only the cutest freshman at King High. And the coolest. He had this tough-looking little body and these blue eyes and this corn-silk hair that was short in back and long on top and swished around the way I always wished my own hair would do . . .

Anyway, the thing was, he didn't know he had it all over Antonio Banderas. He acted like he was this everyday kid, and I loved that about him. I'd started loving it the first time I noticed him in my Spanish class.

Too bad, because he barely knew I was alive. Of course, let's face it, Fletcher was way too good for me. I mean, what honors student is going to look twice at a chick with a learning disability who has to take a special reading class? Not to mention that I wasn't on his social level—well, you get the idea.

So mostly I'd just looked at him from across the classroom and daydreamed a lot. Now I was going to be sitting in the same car with him.

"Cheyenne, are you okay?" Tobey said. She unlocked Lazarus's door for me and stared at me while I piled into the passenger seat with my backpack.

"Sure, why?" I said.

She didn't answer until she climbed into the driver's side and started up the heater. We could see our breath hanging in the air, and the car was likely to stay that cold. You could never count on Lazarus's heater.

"You just keep drifting in and out," she said. "One minute you're with us, the next you're out in Never-Never Land."

"I'm just thinkin' about stuff," I said. "And yes, I *do* think."

She blinked at me before she pulled the car out of the parking space. "I know you do," she said. "I'd never say you didn't."

I shrugged. "It's okay. People have said it before."

"Like who?" she said. "I'll rip their lips off."

"You can't," I said. "It was my ex-stepfather—and he's in jail."

"Oh," she said.

There was this embarrassed silence. People always reacted that way when I told them somebody in my family was doing time. I kept forgetting not everybody lived with that kind of stuff in her past.

"He actually said, 'Oh, you *think!?*'" Tobey said.

"Yeah. I'd say something like, 'I was thinking . . . ,' and he would say, 'Oh, I thought I smelled something burning.' Then he would go on about how I never had a rational thought in my life, ya-da ya-da."

"Nice guy," Tobey said. "But things are better now, right? Now that you're living with Tassie?"

"She never says I'm stupid," I said. "But then, she didn't even graduate from high school." I really wanted to change the subject. That was never hard for me. I could always think of something to say. "So what's Fletcher doing after school this late?"

Tobey smirked. "Detention."

"No way!"

"Yes, way. He was late for English three times. Probably chasing after some girl or something."

"Oh," I said. I might not have been Fletcher's type, but my heart still sagged like a Baggie full of water.

"Ever since last fall when he was helping us," Tobey was saying, "he's been like this—what does he call it—'babe magnet.'" Tobey shuddered. "I hate that expression. Sounds like something Jerry Pavella would say."

"Isn't that one of those guys who tried to get Norie in trouble?"

"Yes. Loser." She looked up. "Sorry, God. Chey, did you know Pavella actually asked Marissa out after all that stuff that went down with Norie?"

"You can't blame him," I said. "She's so pretty and nice."

"And he's so lame. She turned him down, of course."

"She turns everybody down," I said. "Do you think she's scared of guys?"

"If she isn't, she ought to be," Tobey said. "I think Norie and Brianna have the only two decent guys at King. Maybe in Reno." She pulled the car into the King High parking lot and pointed through the windshield. "Including that little joker right there."

She was talking, of course, about Fletcher, who was waiting on the curb in this way cool-looking Australian trench coat that came down to his ankles. It must have cost him $150.

I looked at my down jacket that Tassie had mended the hole in, and I wanted to crawl under the seat. Instead, I scrambled into the back.

"Let him sit back there, Chev," Tobey said.

"That's okay," I said. "I have shorter legs. And besides, it's his car, and he's older. Tassie always lets whoever's oldest sit up front when we go out in the van. Usually that's Ellie, because Diesel has his own truck. He hardly ever rides with us. And I hardly ever ride with him. His truck smells so bad. He says it's transmission fluid, and as soon as he gets the money he's going to have the leak fixed. He'll probably suffocate somebody first."

"Don't you mean 'asphyxiate'?" Fletcher said.

I'd been babbling on so hard—I always did that when I was nervous enough to stop breathing—I hadn't even noticed that he'd climbed in and shut the door, and we were going again.

"Oh yeah," I said.

"Thank you, Mr. Vocabulary," Tobey said. She jabbed him with an elbow as she maneuvered the car around the ice patches. "How was detox?"

"Detention," he said, eyes squinted at her.

Detox. Now there was a word I knew. How many times had my real mother been through it . . . I stuffed that thought and tuned in on Fletcher.

"It was lame," Fletcher was saying. "They made us sit in this room and do our homework like it was some kind of punishment. I did all mine so now I can just kick back tonight." He leaned around the seat and looked at me. "The Spanish homework is really easy," he said. "I was done in about ten minutes."

"Oh," I said. That would come out to about an hour for me. I was such a dork in that class.

"It's just a dialogue," he went on. "*¿Cómo está usted?*"

I waited for him to go on. He looked at me for a second and then did his hands around in circles.

"What?" I said.

"*Cómo está usted?*"

"Oh!" I said. "Uh, *Muy bien, gracias.*" Whew. Close one.

He gave me this really slow grin. It always took him a long time to finish a smile. I thought that was so cool.

"Well?" he said.

"Well what?"

"Aren't you going to ask me how I am?"

"How are ya?" I said.

"No—in *español!*"

What was *español*? Oh, yeah, Spanish. Duh.

"Uh," I said, sounding pretty much like R2-D2. "*¿Y tú?*"

He launched into this way cute Mexican accent. I started to giggle.

"*Soy muy muerte,*" he said.

I am very "something," I thought. *Okay, come on, Cheyenne, don't blow this. Um, ask him why. What's the word for "why"?*

"*¿Por qué?*" I said and hoped I hadn't just said "who" or "dog" or something worse.

Apparently I was on the right track, because he held up both hands, looked totally bummed, and said, "*Yo no tengo amigos.*"

I don't have a yo-yo? I thought frantically. No, that couldn't be it. *Tengo* meant "I have"—I was pretty sure. Or did it mean "I dance"? No, that was *tango. Okay, forget trying to translate. Just go with it before he figures out you're an idiot.*

"*¿Oh?*" I said, sadly—and that was no act. "*¿No aminos?*"

Fletcher let out the biggest belly laugh since Santa left the mall. He snorted and snuffled until Tobey told him to knock it off because he was getting snot on the windshield.

"What's so funny?" I said.

"It isn't *aminos!*" he said. "It's *amigos!* No aminos? I'd be dead!"

"What's aminos?" I said. "I know I've heard it."

"You have—in science class. Amino acids. Ring a bell?"

He kept chuckling. I laughed right along with him.

"Oh," I said. "Duh. I knew that. I did."

"Uh-huh," Fletcher said.

"Shut up, Bozo," Tobey said, "before you slide off the Rude Scale."

Fletcher looked at her innocently with those big blue eyes—between snorts. "I'm not being rude, man," he said. "I think that's funny. I can be your amino, Cheyenne! *¿Hey, mi amino, que pasa, huh?*"

"*¡Sí!*" I said.

It was a lame attempt to leave him thinking I was halfway intelligent. How could you go wrong with "yes"? Evidently I'd found a way, because Fletcher was about to kill himself laughing. All I could think to do was laugh, too, which made him laugh even harder. Dude, I wanted to get out of that car.

"I love you, Cheyenne," Tobey said. Even she was grinning.

"Why?" I said.

"He asks you what's happening, and you say 'yes'! I love it! You are a kick!"

Oh, I'm just a kick in the pants, I thought. *God, please could you get me out of here?!*

When we pulled into our driveway, Fletcher was still laughing. Tobey had to let me out her side.

"I have to get him home," she said to me. "He's about to wet his pants."

"Yeah, me, too," I said absently.

That set him off even more. I could still hear him howling all the way down the street.

Which was why I was in the foulest mood on record when I walked in the front door. It didn't matter that the smell of Tassie's beef stew was all over the house or that she had a fire going in the fireplace or that it was Ellie's turn to set the table and Brendan's to wash dishes. I threw my books under my bed in our room and flopped myself down into my chair at the kitchen table.

Tassie turned from the stove and crossed her arms over

her enormous chest. Avery once told me he thought Tassie had stood in the breast line twice before she was born, and that's why she was so big. Then he had looked at me and said she obviously had taken the ones I was supposed to get. I slugged him, of course.

Anyway, Tassie narrowed her little twinkly blue eyes at me. "Were you plannin' to eat with us?" she said.

I nodded.

"Then here's the sink, and there's the soap," she said.

I sulked all the way to the sink and started to wash my hands.

"Leave some skin on them," Felise said in her gruff voice. Most people on the phone thought she was one of the boys. Even some people in person thought she was one of the boys. She didn't go in too much for makeup and clothes.

Ellie, on the other hand, did nothing but sit in front of the mirror and do her mascara and stuff. She got up an hour earlier than the rest of us just to fix herself up. I'd rather sleep, myself. She always said it showed."

"What's wrong with her?" said a voice from the doorway.

That was Avery. He dragged his feet across the kitchen floor. He always dragged his feet, but when Ellie asked Tassie why she didn't get on him about it, Tassie said he had worse problems she needed to work on. He shoved me aside to get to the soap. I shoved him back—only I wasn't playing.

"Man, who rattled your cage?" he said. He had one of those voices like he always had a sore throat. Probably from cigarettes.

"Nobody," I said. "Just leave me alone."

"Now, Cheyenne, you know better than to say somethin' like that," Diesel said. He was our oldest foster brother and the biggest, being Tassie's real kid and all. Six foot six. Muscles in his arms bigger than the ones in my thighs. I wouldn't have said it to anybody in the family, but he was my favorite.

"Why?" I said.

"Because the minute you ask any of these guys to leave you alone, they're going to be all over you," he said.

He held out a chair for Tassie, and she sat. Avery and Brendan waited until we girls were all sitting before they sat. They hated that, but it was one of Tassie's rules.

"There's no reason you can't be a gentleman," she always said. "And if you're not, I'll pull out your nose hairs with red hot tweezers."

"So what's your problem?" Ellie said to me after the blessing. She tossed her hair back over her shoulders and looked at me from out of the eye makeup. It was a miracle she could even see. Who knew what color her eyes were?

"Nothing," I said.

"Then why aren't you runnin' your mouth like you usually do?" Avery said. He smirked at Brendan, who smirked back. Brendan never said much. He just did whatever Avery did. Weird, too, because he was half again as big and twice as good looking. At least he cut his hair.

"She wants to be left alone," Tassie said. "Respect that."

"She wants us to beg her to tell what's wrong, is what she wants," Ellie said. "Come on, kid, out with it."

Felise grunted and picked up the breadbasket. "Do you really care what's wrong, or are you just bein' nosy?" she said to Ellie.

"Shut up," Ellie said.

"No cake for you tonight," Avery said.

True. We weren't allowed to tell each other to shut up. Ellie was always catching flak for that. But that thought went in and out of my head like a goldfish. The mention of cake reminded me.

"Tassie," I said, "I told the girls you would bake a cake for Brianna's birthday party day after tomorrow."

Tassie set down her fork and looked at me.

Oops. I'd messed something up. Again.

"You *told* them I would?" she said.

Avery started to hum the funeral march.

"Yeah," I said.

"You didn't *ask* me first? You just assumed I would?"

"Yeah, I guess so," I said. I started to get nervous. "Won't you?" I said.

"I will—because I like those girls," Tassie said. "But I want to be asked first before you go volunteering me. I do have things to do, you know."

"Yeah, like bake cakes for *us*," Avery said.

Ellie told him to shut up—with her eyes. After all, she had already lost dessert.

"You just button your lip and listen up, Avery," Tassie said. "We could all use a lesson in not taking each other for granted."

"I don't take you for granted, Tassie," Avery said. "I lo-o-o-ve you!" He got this innocent look in his little, yellow-brown eyes.

Didn't fool her for a second. She picked up her fork again and stabbed at her potatoes. "Is that why you were still hangin' out across the street with all those smokers before school and lunchtime instead of finding some decent people to run around with?"

"What's that got to do with me taking you for granted?" Avery said.

"The minute you get in trouble, you know they're going to snatch you right out of here," Tassie said, without blinking an eye. "You think I can do anything about that, you and Brendan?"

Brendan raised his gray eyes for a second and then looked back at his plate and fiddled with his earring. Of course he hung out across the street with Avery. I sometimes wondered if he would know when to go to the bathroom if it wasn't for Avery.

"You'd bail us out, you know you would, Tassie," Avery said. He shook his mousy-brown hair out of his face and grinned at her. Too bad he had crooked teeth in the front. He would be kind of cute in a pet-mouse way if it weren't for that.

"I am not the judge and jury in this town," Tassie said. "Some things are out of my control. Only one in control right now is you. You can either hang out with those I-don't-give-a-hang types and run the risk of getting yourself in trouble, or you can find you some healthy friends. I can't pick your friends for you."

They went on, bantering back and forth. I let out a long, slow breath. At least the spotlight was off me. Tassie always said Avery and Brendan were her hard-core cases. My volunteering her to bake a cake was nothing compared to the stuff they could get into at the drop of a ball cap.

But my problems still seemed pretty big to me. I spent my required hour in the homework room. That's this little room at the back of the house that used to be a screened-in porch. Tassie had it closed in and used it as a study hall for us. We had to work in there for an hour or until our homework was done. She had card tables set up and a couch I loved to curl up on, even though the stuffing was oozing out, and she let us play music low. She said it was conductive—no, Norie said it was conducive—to learning.

But I couldn't concentrate that night. I halfway did my stuff, but as soon as my hour was over, I escaped to our room, the one I shared with Ellie and Felise.

We each had a bed that was up about six feet from the floor so that underneath was a space we could use for whatever we wanted. Ellie had a dressing table and a makeup mirror in hers. Felise had a drawing board set up so she could do her art thing. She had painted a mural on our wall—wolves howling at the moon. It was cool.

Until recently I hadn't known what to do with my space. When Norie taught me to listen to God for ten minutes and then write down everything I thought I heard, I asked Tassie to give me this big floor pillow nobody ever sat on in the living room, and I stuck it under there with my notebook. I draped my sheets down real low like a curtain so I could go in there and have privacy. I went there that night and tried to listen.

Sometimes I'd actually thought I heard God. For instance, in December, when Norie had been in trouble and I was the only one who could get her out of it, I felt God had basically told me what to do.

So why isn't He talking now? I wondered as I sat on the pillow and then lay on the floor with my head on it. Then did a tripod upside down on it. That was how Tassie found me when she knocked on the door.

"You got time to talk?" she asked from the doorway.

I tumbled upright and pulled back my "curtain."

She hauled her wonderful, big body in there with me, and I gave her the pillow to sit on.

"I have to get some furniture in here," I said. "Next time Ethan Allen has a sale—you know, I'll pick up a few leather couches and maybe a big entertainment center."

Her blue eyes twinkled, and she shook her head, which was covered in pure white hair even though she wasn't near old enough for it. She said it had turned gray when she was twenty-five and white by the time she was forty. She had it cut in a bob that made her look younger—and besides, to me she *was* young. How many adults do you know who will fly kites, play soccer, and stay up till midnight trying to beat you in backgammon?

She was still shaking her head at me. "I never saw the likes of you, girl," she said. "You can talk longer than anybody can listen to you and about nothin'. Then the minute you really need to open up, you dodge the truth like it's a Mack truck coming at you. Now why don't you hush about furniture and tell me what's botherin' you."

"Nothing's bothering me," I said.

"And I'm going to be on the cover of *Cosmo* next month," Tassie said. "Come on, honey, this is me you're talking to. What's on your mind?"

I made my first dodge. "I'm sorry about the cake," I said.

"No harm done. You'll ask first next time," she said. "Tomorrow we'll talk about what you want on it. Brianna's the one who's an artist, isn't she?"

I nodded, but Tassie kept looking at me.

"What else?" she said.

It was no use. Short of making up something, which she would see right through anyway, I might as well spill my guts or we would be there all night. The reason Tassie could set kids straight was that she was more stubborn than your basic mule. I gave this big ol' sigh, and she started to smile. She knew I'd given up.

"I don't have a present for Brianna," I said. "I know you're going to say that's stupid—"

"I beg your pardon, Cheyenne Jackson," Tassie said, drawing herself up to full sitting height. "I have never said that something you thought was stupid, now have I?"

"No," I said.

"All right, then. Forget what I think and tell me what *you* think."

"I think I hate it that I don't have any money to buy her a gift. I'm just not like the Flagpole Girls even though they're nice to me, which is probably only because they have to be. I mean, why should they hang out with me? I'm in the dumb classes. I dress in stuff they would give away to Goodwill. I don't have a boyfriend and probably never will because I'm like a *dog* compared to all of them, and . . ."

I didn't add the part about not having a real family like they did. I do control my mouth once in a while.

As I paused, I saw Tassie was thinking. I could see it in her eyes, the way they looked right at me, into me, through me, and out the other side with the answers.

"Well," she said finally, "most of that stuff you can't do a thing about. All's you can do is pray. But you can change one thing, and I think you ought to concentrate on that."

"What is it?" I said.

"You can *make* a present for Brianna."

If my heart had lifted at all, it sank like a stone at that point. That sounded like about the dorkiest thing yet. All I had to do was show up with some cat made out of Play-Doh or something and I would prove I was Geek of the Year.

Tassie reached over and touched one of my earrings, which was dangling against my cheek. "You make this beautiful jewelry," she said. "I get compliments on those earrings you made me for Christmas every time I wear them. Why don't you make a set for Brianna?"

I hugged my knees and stared at my feet. "I don't even have the money to buy the beads."

"Hmm," she said.

The part of me that is always just a little hopeful—I think they call it "naive"—thought maybe she was going to give me some money or offer me a chore around the house that she would pay me for. No such luck. Instead, she dropped a bomb on me. A major bomb.

"There's somethin' else I come in here to talk to you about," she said. "We might as well get this out of the way now."

My chest pinched. I couldn't even ask her what it was. Her face was all serious.

"I got a call from the court today," she said. "About your mother."

I could barely breathe. This was one subject I did *not* want to hear about. I'd rather discuss Play-Doh animals.

"She's out of rehab," Tassie said. "Passed with flying colors, finally. They say she's showing signs of being off booze for good."

I didn't believe a word of it. I'd heard enough promises from my mother to fill the Brownie Scout manual. And she had never kept one of them.

Tassie watched me for a second, and then she went on.

"They've sent her to a halfway house. They'll help her make the transition back into real life. That was always the problem before, you see, they would just dry her out and toss her back out on the street. But she didn't know how to live sober."

I didn't answer. The squeezing in my chest wouldn't let me talk.

"It's Robinson House, right here in Reno," Tassie said. "And she's allowed to contact you. I have a feeling you're going to be hearin' from her real soon. Might just be a letter, maybe a phone call."

It was all I could do not to cover up my ears so I wouldn't hear any more. I just nodded.

Tassie kept watching me for a few more minutes, and then she started to crawl out from under my bed. "I think I've loaded you down enough for one night," she said. "Now I'm going to say my three favorite words to you."

"I know," I said. " 'I love you.' "

Tassie eased out of my little cave and picked up something she had set outside it on her way in. Still grinning, with the gap where she was missing a front tooth looking black in the dark room, she shook her head.

"No," she said. " 'Have a cookie.' "

She handed me a plate piled with oatmeal-raisin cookies. When I took it, she leaned back in and gave me a kiss on the cheek.

After she was gone, I set down the plate. I couldn't eat even one of them, good as they smelled. They would have turned to sawdust in my mouth.

No, just then, I couldn't think about eating. All I could think about was my mother's face. Puffed up, bags under her eyes, her hair greasy and pulled back from her forehead. It had been a while since I'd seen her in my mind's eye. I'd been able to cut her out.

But suddenly there she was again. And it hurt. As if things weren't bad enough already, she had to come back into my life.

I curled up on the pillow with my back to the room and squeezed my eyes shut.

No, I wasn't havin' it. I didn't care what it took; I wasn't letting my mother back in.

THE NEXT MORNING I WAS SUPPOSED TO GET EXTRA help from Mr. Hopkins, my math teacher, before school. I didn't do it.

I'd actually been doing better in that class since December when I worked some with Norie's tutor. I was passing now—surprise, and Mr. Hopkins said with some extra help I might even bring my grade up to a *B*. That would be, like, the first *B* I ever got. In anything.

But that morning, with the sky steel gray and the air so cold it almost turned solid in front of you when you breathed and with what Tassie had told me now frozen into my brain, I started to think, *What's the point?*

Really, I mean, why bust my tail, as Avery would have put it, when I was never going to have the kind of life my Flagpole friends did? My mother had seen to that with the childhood she had dragged me through. As far as I could tell, God had yet to answer any—okay, many—of my prayers for the future. Pretty obviously it was going to be more of the same. Same gray. Same cold. Same hopes freezing solid right before my eyes.

All right, all right, so I was feeling sorry for myself. Sorry enough to stand on the front steps of King High School with my hand on the door handle and not to go in there and try.

I turned around and looked across the school grounds. The front lawn, which somehow they managed to keep almost green even in the winter, rolled down to the teachers' parking lot, broken up only by one sidewalk and the flagpole. The same flagpole I'd stood under in September with five girls I didn't know . . .

Nope. I wasn't going there right now. Stubbornly I trained my eyes on the street in front of the school, where all the Jeep Grand Cherokees, Dodge Ram pickups, and BMW sedans were pulling up, dropping off kids from Caughlin Ranch and the Foothills. None of them had ever ridden a jam-packed school bus or a truck that smelled like transmission fluid.

Beyond them was the vacant lot. Even in the below-freezing cold, a bunch of kids were huddled over there. The "I-don't-give-a-hang kids" Tassie had called them. They were like a blob of flannels and ski caps with a cloud of cigarette smoke floating overhead. I knew Avery and Brendan were in there, although it was hard to tell them apart from everybody else.

Suddenly that sounded like a good thing, you know? At least they were all dressed like me. Over there, I'd never notice that my clothes were bought at Kmart because theirs were, too. Over there, it wouldn't make any difference that I wasn't in honors classes, my mother wasn't a Booster, and I didn't have a dime to my name. Over there, we were all the same.

The idea of wriggling myself into the circle and looking like everybody else for a change was the most depressing thing I could think of. And yet it sounded kind of comfortable, too.

I stuck my hands into my overall pockets, lowered my head against the biting wind, and made my way through the Beamers and Suburbans in the parking lot.

I'm not going to smoke, I told myself. *I'm just going to stand there. And nobody's going to ask me if I did my homework, or if I bought Brianna a present, or—*

But my thoughts were interrupted by a tooting horn. I looked up at the edge of the street and stopped. Good thing.

A car was right in front of me. Not a BMW. But a truck. Shiny, red, and new. Diesel would have been able to give the make, model, and engine size.

The frosty window on the passenger side came down, and Brianna leaned her head out. Her nostrils were flared.

"Where do you think you're going, girl?" she said.

"Nowhere," I said automatically. I knew better than to confess. She had that you-better-not-be-messing-up look in her eyes.

"Uh-huh," she said. She pushed open the door. "Get yourself in here. And I don't want to hear any argument."

She slid into the middle, next to her boyfriend, Ira. He nodded at me as I climbed in and closed the door behind me. Cars were blowing their horns, but Ira slowly pulled on and ignored them. Most guys would have cussed or given some kind of hand signal. Not Ira. He was cool all the way.

Brianna made up for it by exploding. "You were going across that street over to those losers, weren't you, girl?" she said. Make that "yelled."

"Sort of," I said.

"What do you mean 'sort of'? You either were, or you weren't. It's just like you can't be 'sort of' pregnant."

"I'm not pregnant!" I said.

"No, but you could end up that way or worse if you get mixed up with that crowd. I *know*, girl. Now tell me what you were thinking of? Why would you think you have to get in with people like that?"

Ira pulled the pickup into a parking space, and Brianna nodded for him to go on. He kissed her on the cheek and got out. It immediately started to turn cold, but Brianna didn't seem to care about that. She didn't take her eyes off me. I mean, dude, I didn't have any choice but to answer—with the truth.

"I think I fit in better over there," I said, staring at my knees.

"Look at me, girl," she said.

I did. Her face was serious.

"You fit in better with a bunch of no-counts than with us?" she said.

I nodded.

"How do you figure that?" she said.

"Because a lot of those kids are in my classes, and they live in my neighborhood. Avery and Brendan do, obviously, since they live in my same house, and I just figured—"

"Girl, you better start telling me the truth, or I tell you what, I'm going to pry it out of you. And if I have to get Norie and Tobey in here, you're going to be sorry you didn't just get right down to it from the start."

I pulled my hands up into the sleeves of my flannel, but that was all the hiding I was going to get away with, I knew that. "I just feel like I'm not like you and Tobey and Norie and all them," I said. "You're all smart and have money and real families. I just feel out of it. I can't even buy—"

I stopped and bit my lip. But Brianna had heard enough. She slung her arm across the back of the seat and put her face about an inch from mine. "Now you listen here," she said. "All you're doing is feeling sorry for your sweet self, and I want you to stop it right now. 'Cause I'll tell you what, that is nothing but the easy way out."

"Easy sounds pretty good right now."

"Yeah, well, you won't think so down the line. Not when you get yourself in some kind of trouble and you don't have anybody to help you out." She punched my shoulder softly with her gloved fist. "Why do you think I made Ira stop this car when I saw you about to cross that street?"

I shrugged.

"Don't give me that," she said. "You know why. Because I give a flip about you. There's no way I'm going to watch you throw yourself away when you've come so far."

For the first time I stopped trying to lower my eyes and looked at her hopefully.

"Is that true?" I said.

"Would I have said it if it wasn't?"

I had to grin. "No," I said.

"All right then. And don't you think for one minute that if you called that crowd over there your friends that they would lift one finger if you got into trouble. They would be too busy running the other way so they wouldn't get caught, too. Mmm-mmm, girl, you better know when you got something good going and stick with it. You understand me?"

I did. And it gave me this warm rush that made me forget I was about to freeze to death. I started to nod like one of those dashboard things on a spring. Diesel had one shaped like a hula dancer . . .

Brianna grabbed me and hugged me really tight. "All right now," she said. "Don't you even be thinking about that nonsense, and if you do, you come right to me or Tobey or Marissa or somebody, you hear?"

"Okay," I said.

She let go of me and straightened my bangs with her fingers. "Come on," she said. "We have to get to class. Did you do your homework last night?"

"No," I said. "But I'll get it done, I promise."

"What were you doing last night?" she said.

"Feeling sorry for myself," I said.

"Well, there isn't going to be any more of that," she said. "We all expect more out of you, girl."

That was all it took. I raced into the school and to my locker like a girl with a mission. You didn't argue with Brianna.

Nor did I want to. She cared about me. That was pretty obvious. I mean, she wouldn't have gone to all that trouble if it didn't make a difference to her what happened to me. I still couldn't see why. I was a freshman; she was a senior. She was beautiful and mature. I was . . .

Anyway, that didn't matter. What mattered was, well, two things. One, they expected more of me, the Flagpole Girls.

They expected me to be one of them. I had to try harder. I had to.

And, two, Brianna had just saved me from making a major stupid mistake. I owed her something now. Like a birthday present.

Come on, God, I prayed as I slid into my desk in English. *Just help me find a way, okay?*

The Flagpole Girls didn't always meet for lunch—only on Fridays officially. But I always checked the theater lobby at lunchtime because usually a few of us would hang out there, just to be together. That was where Ms. Race did her lunch duty, too, so she kept little "jackals," as Norie called them, from harassing us about being Jesus freaks. We usually ended up praying, and these taggers and stoners loved to come through and yell insults while we had our heads bowed. Ms. Race was kind of like this protective angel or something.

Anyway, that day I was praying that some of the girls would be there, and they were—Tobey, Norie, and Ms. Race. I made an immediate note that none of the boys was there. Okay, I noticed that Fletcher wasn't there. Bummer. But I skidded in with my brown bag lunch, and Tobey immediately offered me some celery sticks with peanut butter that her mother had packed.

"I hate celery," she said.

I swapped her for two of Tassie's oatmeal-raisin cookies and tuned in on the conversation that was already in progress.

"We want some really cool stores," Norie was saying. "Some places where we can get out-of-the-ordinary stuff for Brianna."

Ms. Race wrinkled her nose real cute the way she did when she smiled. "So for out-of-the-ordinary you came to me, my being a freak and all."

"No!" Tobey said. She got all flustered. She wouldn't insult Saddam Hussein.

"I'm just teasing you," Ms. Race said. She fingered her auburn French braid like she was thinking. "I guess the best place to send you is that obscure little strip mall down on Plumb Lane. It's across from that big auto parts store. Grand Theft Auto or whatever it is."

"It's just Grand Auto," Norie said, snorting. "Shops are over there?"

"They're tucked way back off the road," Ms. Race said. "There's a bead store and a—"

"Bead store?" I said. "Dude!"

"Oh, that's right," Ms. Race said. She nodded at my necklace. "I forgot you're into jewelry-making. They have beautiful things, Cheyenne. Are you thinking about something like that for Brianna?"

"Oh, definitely. She's so into jewelry. Forget clothes . . . like I could tell her how to dress? But now, jewelry, that's kind of my thing . . ."

Where I was going to get the money I still didn't know, but this was sounding better. If Ms. Race didn't think it would be dorky to make Brianna something, it must be okay.

"You want to come with us, Chey?" Tobey said. "Norie and I are going shopping after school."

"Me?" I said.

"No," Norie said. "She was talking to that little tagger over there who's about to pull the fire alarm."

Ms. Race stood up smoothly, and her boots clicked across the tile. "I don't think so," she said to the kid in this calm voice.

Norie poked me. "Of course you," she said. "Meet us at my locker."

The feeling you get when you're invited to do something with people you think are right up there with the angels and Matthew McConaughey or somebody—that stayed with me until I was on my way to fifth period. Then I started to panic.

Okay, I thought, *so they want me to go with them. But what am I supposed to do for money? Am I going to just stand there looking like a loser while they fork over the cash for these big, elaborate presents?*

That pinched at my chest as I rounded the corner to the lockers. So much so I forgot to look for Fletcher. Suddenly he was there, right in my path.

"Hi," he said with about half a smile. "I brought you a present." Then he dropped a crumpled up Doritos bag into my hand and walked off, leaving me with one word shouting at me from what he had said: "present."

I had to find a way.

I went to class by way of auto shop. Diesel had three periods in there; so he was greasy from fingers to chin—and he didn't look happy to see me.

"What's up?" he said. "I'm trying to adjust a carburetor."

"Diesel," I said. And then I swallowed. "Do you have any money I could have?"

He looked at me as if I'd just asked for the keys to his precious truck. It wasn't a pretty look.

"Never mind," I said. "It was stupid. Just forget it."

I turned on my heel and headed for the door, nearly knocking over some big greasy thing with a lot of moving parts.

"Hey, get away from my transmission!" somebody yelled.

I felt a grab at my arm, which left a black handprint I was probably never going to get off, since Diesel never seemed to . . .

"Wait," Diesel said.

He let go of my arm and dug around in his jeans pocket, which was no small feat since, unlike Brendan and Avery, he wore his pants skintight.

"Here," he said and handed me two dollars. I think they were dollars. They matched his fingers, if you know what I'm saying.

I felt like I was going to cry. "Thanks, Diesel!" I said. "I'll pay you back, I promise!"

"How? Did you suddenly get a job when I wasn't looking? Forget it. You can do my dishes one night or something."

"I'll do them two nights—three!" I said.

"Get out of here," he said. "You're going to be late for class, and they'll call the house, and Ma will blow a gasket."

I got out, clutching the two grimy dollar bills like they were the crown jewels. At the moment, it didn't matter that it was probably enough for about half an earring. That didn't matter until *after* we had left school that afternoon and Norie pulled into Wendy's and said, "I'm starving."

Then I made my next stupid move. I mean, I couldn't just stand there while they ordered. I got some fries and a small Coke. And had sixteen cents left over.

Then it mattered.

The first store we went into was definitely neat. Not only did they have some of the most gorgeous beads I'd ever seen, but there also was a bunch of other cool things. Norie found a leather-bound sketchbook. It looked like it was made for Brianna. And Tobey, after she looked at and picked up everything in the place, decided on a belt with all this rad stitching and grommets and all. I knew Brianna had about three outfits that would go perfect with.

Me, I stood in front of the beads display and just about drooled. I could have made a dozen pairs of earrings to go with Brianna's wardrobe. She wore deep, rich colors, and they had great, tear-shaped tiger-eyes and smoky-gray empress cut beads that would have matched so well.

I designed one pair in my mind. The teardrops hanging below the gray glass beads held by gold hooks, and they even had twenty-four karat gold fittings to put them on. I could close my eyes and see them against Brianna's skin. She was golden, they were golden. It was like art or something.

"You coming, Cheyenne?" somebody said beside me.

I shook my head at Tobey. My heart was racing, I was getting so panicked.

"I'm still looking," I said.

"We'll go next door and browse then," Norie said from the end of the aisle.

"Oh, they have nice things in there," said the lady behind her.

She was the shopkeeper, and she reminded me of a softer version of Tassie. She had gray, almost white hair, and she wore it in a big, thick braid piled on top of her head. She was round, sort of cuddly looking, and she had been smiling at us ever since we came in. A lot of places you go, they don't smile at teenagers.

"Just come over when you're done," Tobey said to me.

I nodded numbly as they left, and the shopkeeper went back to her counter. Then I looked at the beads again.

What am I going to do? my head was screaming at me. *I need these for Brianna. I'm going to look like a total loser if I show up without a present for her after what she did for me this morning. God, what am I supposed to do?*

Whatever it was I was supposed to do, God didn't tell me. It definitely wasn't Him telling me to scoop up the beads and the fittings I wanted and shove them into the pockets of my overalls.

But I heard it from somewhere.

And that's exactly what I did.

CHAPTER THREE

THEN I STOOD THERE WITH MY CHEST SQUEEZING IN. I didn't move because I couldn't. I was frozen to the floor with a bunch of stolen beads in my pockets. I don't know what I would have done if the phone hadn't rung and jangled me into motion.

Vaguely I heard the shopkeeper answer it. She would be busy for a minute. Willing myself to go slow, I put one foot in front of the other and reached the door. To my pounding brain, it was a miracle that it opened; that I got outside; that no one tackled me, threw me to the ground, and clamped handcuffs on my wrists.

I was outside. I was walking away. I was looking back through the glass door.

Why I looked, I'll never know. I call it God. Because as I did, the shopkeeper looked back at me.

And she smiled.

And she waved.

Just like I was another satisfied customer she had sent away happy. There she was, looking at me with her angel face and her trusting eyes. It twisted my chest into a knot.

"Hey!"

I jumped like a shot squirrel. But it was only Tobey, grinning at my elbow.

"You ready?" she said.

"Yeah," I said.

"Are you freezing?" Norie said. "You're shaking. Get her to the car, L'Orange, before she turns into an icicle."

"Why didn't you wear a coat?" Tobey said.

Because it's got a stupid mended hole in it, I thought.

It only took a minute for Norie's Jeep—Iggy, she called him—to warm up, but my teeth were still chattering. I wondered if I'd ever stop shaking. Even looking back as we pulled out of the parking lot and seeing that nobody was running out of the bead store with a shotgun didn't slow me down. Only one thing did.

"I'm sorry you didn't find what you wanted, Cheyenne," Tobey said from the front seat.

"What?" I said.

"I said I'm sorry you didn't find anything for Brianna. Will you be able to go back out tonight?"

"I did get something!" I said.

I watched both their faces, but neither of them looked suspicious. Norie didn't even glance at me in the rearview mirror.

"What did you get?" Tobey said.

I reached into my pockets, and then I froze again. Were they going to wonder when I pulled out beads with no store bag?

I left my hand in there. "I want it to be a surprise," I said. "You'll see tomorrow when I give them to her."

"Give us a hint," Norie said.

"I'm making her some earrings," I said.

"That wasn't a hint," Norie said, snorting. "That was the answer!"

"You're going to make them?" Tobey said. "That's so cool. I wish I had some artistic talent. If I made something for Brianna, she could use it to scare off snakes."

"Same here," Norie said. "I made those posters for everybody for Christmas, but I know they weren't, like, ready for prime-time viewing or anything."

"Oh yeah," I said. I'd forgotten about that, and I'd loved that Norie had made them. I had mine in my cave. "You really think it's okay that I'm making her jewelry instead of buying it at like Zales or something?" I said.

"Are you kidding?" Tobey reached back and squeezed my knee. "Brianna would hate jewelry from Zales. She's going to freak. I'm totally jealous."

That was all I needed to hear. It was enough to drive the Angel Lady out of my head and to keep me up half the night making the masterpiece earrings. I even had enough beads left over to decorate a card. I wasn't sure I'd spelled everything right on it, but by the time I finished it everybody else was asleep. That was okay. I'd ask Shannon the next day. She did everything perfect.

Yeah, I was riding high, and I kept on through the next day. It was an awesome day, too.

I convinced Diesel to drive me to school so the cake wouldn't get trashed on the bus. It was hard enough keeping Avery from sticking his fingers into it. Tassie had put a painter's palette on it with frosting and made these little drops that looked like paint splashes down from it. I wasn't letting anybody mess it up.

"Chill, will you?" Avery said to me when I gave him my best dagger eyes. "Who's going to miss a little icing?"

"I am," I said, teeth gritted together. "So keep your dirty, scummy, sticky fingers off it."

"Any more questions?" Diesel said.

After I gave the cake to Ms. Race in the office to keep, I tore over to the senior locker hall where everybody was pulling balloons out of a garbage bag in front of Brianna's locker.

"Are all those going in there?" I said.

"What doesn't fit we can tie on the front," Marissa said. "I have some extra ribbon."

"I love it!" Tobey said. She loved everything. And I loved her—and everybody. I was in that kind of mood.

Shannon put her armful of balloons in the locker and stepped back shyly. I remembered what I had to ask her.

"Would you check my card for spelling?" I whispered to her.

"Sure," she said.

I pulled it carefully out of my backpack, and she gasped, like she was about to have an asthma attack.

"What's wrong?" I said. My chest started to pinch.

"Nothing. This is just gorgeous!" Shannon said.

"What is?" Norie said.

She elbowed her way in and before I knew it, everybody was gathered around looking at my card.

"Yikes," Norie said. "That is rad."

"Did you make it, Cheyenne?" Marissa said.

I nodded. Four pairs of impressed eyes looked at me.

"I'm not worthy," Tobey said. "I mean it. My card is this dinky little Hallmark I picked out. I could never do that."

"Wait till you see the earrings," I said.

It sounded a little like bragging, but I was on a roll. Nobody seemed to mind. Norie jabbed me with her finger. "I want to see them now."

"Nope," I said. "They're already wrapped."

"If they're anything like this," Shannon said, tapping the card, "they're beautiful. I can't wait to see them."

And I couldn't wait for her to. It was the best I'd felt . . . well, maybe my whole life, I wasn't sure. It surrounded me with this glow, this "in" glow.

It only got better after third period when we gathered at the locker. Brianna was a creature of habit. She always went to her locker after third. Only today we were all there, and we burst into "Happy Birthday" the minute she turned the corner. She would have run, I know, if Ira hadn't caught her and made her stand in front of us while we howled out the words. She couldn't help it; she grinned this big smile from earlobe to earlobe. I found myself imagining the earrings on those lobes. They were going to look spectacular . . .

"I don't even have to ask if it was you all who put the balloons in my locker this morning," Brianna said when we finished.

"Who else?" Tobey said.

"You are evil!" Brianna said. But she was still smiling. I even thought she looked like she might cry in a minute. Brianna wasn't the crying kind.

"What are you doing for lunch?" Marissa said.

"No, it's 'here's what you *are* doing for lunch,'" Norie said. "You're meeting us in the theater lobby."

"I am?" Brianna said.

Ira nodded. "You are."

"Let me guess. Twenty or thirty of my most intimate friends will be there."

"You got it," Tobey said. "Don't be late."

"She won't," Ira said.

Brianna searched the group, and her eyes fell on me. "What are they planning, Cheyenne? You'll tell me, won't you?"

"No way!" I said.

"Girl, if I can't get it out of you, who am I going to turn to?"

"Forget it, Brianna," I said. "You could do those bamboo things under my fingernails, you could give me that Japanese drippy thing, what is it?"

"Chinese water torture?" Tobey said.

"Yeah. Only I could never figure out why water dropping on your head would be so bad—"

"Cheyenne," Norie said, "stop before you hurt yourself."

I did, and I grinned at Brianna till my face hurt. I really was special to her. This was worth it. Even the stealing—a fact I immediately buried so I could go on with my awesome day.

When lunchtime finally arrived, I was the first one to the theater lobby with the cake and the earrings. Fletcher was the second, pushing this huge box he could have fit into himself.

I, of course, was suddenly nervous and started to chatter like a chimpanzee. Good grief, I was a dork.

"What's that?" I said. "Are you going to climb in there and jump out and be Brianna's present?"

At least I didn't add that that was a present *I* would have died for.

"No, I don't think Ira would like that," he said. "It's my present for her though. It's lame."

"No way," I said. "It couldn't be lame."

"How do you know?" he said, starting that slow smile. "You don't even know what it is."

"What is it?"

"A bicycle."

My mouth dropped open to my belly button. He had bought Brianna a bicycle? I got the only real pinch I'd had in my chest all day. My earrings might be beautiful, but they couldn't compete with a bicycle. These people must be made of twenty-dollar bills.

Fletcher kept smiling at me. "You don't think it's lame?" he said.

I shook my head. But what did it matter what I thought? Oh well.

The rest of the group arrived then, including Diesel and Wyatt, who was kind of like Norie's boyfriend, and they were all laughing and hugging on each other and me. Then Ira got there with Brianna, blindfolded, and it was such a hoot I forgot to think about anything else. Everybody about had a coronary over the cake, even Brianna who just didn't get that excited about stuff. Then we opened presents.

I have to say, she really did have tears in her eyes when she opened my earrings. There was this major gasp when she held them up, too.

"You made those, Cheyenne?" Shannon said.

"Uh-huh," I said.

"I am majorly impressed," Norie said.

Everybody else said the same thing. Brianna put them on right away, and then she came across the circle and gave me this big ol' tight hug.

"I wouldn't be able to stand it if you weren't one of us, girl," she whispered in my ear.

"I wouldn't either," I whispered back.

When she backed away, I caught Diesel from across the circle looking at me.

Uh-oh, I thought. *He's going to start asking questions.*

But he didn't. He just gave me a thumbs up and then focused on Brianna tearing open Fletcher's big box.

What does he know about what beads cost? I thought. *He probably thinks I spent the two dollars he gave me for the stuff.*

Yeah, it was going to be all right.

"Oh, my gosh!" Brianna cried.

She pulled down the last side of the box and was staring with her hands over her mouth.

"Whoa," Norie said. "Somebody spent some bucks."

"No, I didn't," Fletcher said. He looked at Brianna almost like he was ashamed or something.

"Tobey said you had always wanted a bike when you were a kid, and you never got one."

"Right," she said. "We lived in a big city, and my mama wouldn't hear of it."

"We never used this one anymore, so I painted it and fixed it up for you." Fletcher gave his slow smile, like he had just decided not to be ashamed. "It didn't cost me a cent!"

"I love that!" Ms. Race said. "Good for you, Fletcher!"

"No, he's just a cheapskate," Tobey said. Then she and Fletcher punched each other.

I guess. I zoned out.

He didn't spend a cent, and they all think it's wonderful. What's that about?

I didn't get to answer myself. Somebody was tugging at my sleeve.

"Hey," Fletcher said.

I tried not to start blabbering. I mean, dude, I really tried.

"I'm thinking about getting my ear pierced," he said.

"Oh, you are not!" Tobey said.

"How do you know what I'm thinking?" he said. "I am!"

"Cool," Diesel said.

"I know where you can get it done cheap," Ira said. He tugged at the gold ball on his earlobe.

"I can see it all now," Tobey said. "Dad would have a cow!"

Fletcher ignored her. "Hey, so I'm thinking, my amino here, she could make me an earring!"

"Your amino?" Norie said. "What's he talking about?"

"Forget it," Tobey said.

"So how 'bout it?" Fletcher said to me.

I forced myself to smile. "Sure!" I said. "What color do you want?"

"What do you think? Purple maybe?"

I had no idea. All I could think about was—well, about a hundred things. That Fletcher L'Orange was paying attention to me. That it would be really cool if I could make him this neat present. And that, if I did, I was going to have to rip off the lady with the angel face again.

"If you're done pawin' her, boy," I heard Brianna say, "I need to talk to her."

"Go for it," Fletcher said. He drifted away, and Brianna took hold of my arm, like she had a really good reason to hold on to it.

"Where are we going?" I said, as she steered me toward the hall.

"Just right out here," she said. "I have something to ask you."

I tried to breathe. I tried not to look as scared as I suddenly felt.

It was a bust. I couldn't do anything when she stopped out in the hall by the water fountain and got right in my face. "All right, I think you better tell me, girl," she said.

"Tell you what?"

"You better tell me where you got the money for these beads."

CHAPTER FOUR

MY FACE MAY HAVE LOOKED LIKE I WAS GOING INTO a coma, but my mind was going out of control. *She knows! She figured it out!*

Her eyes had gone down to slits, and she was drumming her fingernails against the wall. My mouth went dry. Of course. All the moisture was suddenly in the palms of my hands.

"We're going to stand here till you answer me, girl," Brianna said.

I believed that. Her lips were set in an iron line, and her nostrils were flaring so wide I could have crawled into one of them. I wanted to crawl in somewhere. She was scaring me. I put my hand up to my chest and hung on to the front of my T-shirt as she kept looking at me. Julius, my stepfather, used to give me power stares, but none of them had ever made me as terrified as hers did right then. Probably because I cared what *she* thought.

I opened my mouth, but nothing came out. Brianna brought her lips into a bunch. "Don't pull that with me," she said. "I have never known you to be at a loss for words. Come on, what did you do?"

I honestly tried to say it. I just couldn't. She got her face so close to mine I could smell her lip gloss. "Did you use your lunch money, girl?" she said into my nose. "Or some cash

Tassie gave you to buy school supplies? You been going without binder paper or something?"

"It's no big deal," I managed to get out of my mouth. "They look great on you though. I mean, I'm not bragging or anything, I just think—"

I stopped because Brianna was shaking her head. "I know you don't have much money, Cheyenne," she said. "So don't try to tell me you didn't sacrifice something to buy me a birthday present. I know how you are. You'd give your last dime for somebody else."

It finally dawned on me what she was saying. I told you, I'm not too quick about stuff like that. She wasn't accusing me of stealing. She was thinking I'd given up something to save the money.

I was so relieved I actually laughed. I felt the way you do when you come out of the bathroom at Wittenberg where a bunch of girls have been smoking and you know you smell like smoke even though you weren't doing it, and you think the warden is going to bust you, too, and then she doesn't.

Well, you get the idea. All I could do was blurt out these big, relieved giggles until Brianna put her hands up and said, "All right, forget it, girl. It can't be anything too bad or you wouldn't be standing there about to laugh yourself sick."

I shook my head again and kept laughing. Brianna toyed with one of the new earrings while she inspected me some more. I'd been right: They really did look great on her. Sophisticated. I'd actually done something sophisticated.

"Just don't you do it again," she said.

I tripped over my tongue. "Don't do what?" I said.

"Don't be forking over your last nickel for gifts. We have you, and that's plenty. You hear what I'm sayin'?"

"Yeah," I said.

I was still grinning, but it had turned to plastic. By the time she met Ira at the corner and disappeared into the after-lunch mob in the hall, I was sure my face was stuck that way. And all the merriment had gone out of it. Out of me.

She thought I was so good, such a total Christian, that I'd made some kind of supreme sacrifice for her birthday present. And all I'd done was steal it.

I stood there against the wall while the hordes passed me on their way to fifth period. They might as well have been a firing squad, that's how guilty I knew I must have looked.

I'm just a punk, I thought. *I'm just this total thief, waiting for somebody to find me out.*

Two freshman girls in Gap wardrobes looked at me just then, and I thought for one wild second that I'd said it out loud. But they both wrinkled up their foreheads and made their eyes go real wide, you know, the you-are-a-freak look, and rolled their eyes at each other. It was one of those "whatever" moments that makes you feel like a complete loser.

You don't even know! I wanted to scream after them. *There was no other way! And I'm never going to do it again!*

They had probably moved on to the next putdown of the next poor lowlife they saw in the hall, but I was still defending myself in my mind. *For half a day I felt like everybody else,* I wanted to shout. *For about the first time in my whole, stupid life. That's why I did it!*

I guess in a way I'm grateful I had that half a day. Because I wasn't going to feel good again for a long, long time. Being a shoplifter was only half of it.

I avoided the Flagpole Girls for the rest of the day, just to be on the safe side. I was sure one look at my face and any of them could have testified against me in a court of law. Okay, so maybe I'd watched too many cop shows. Anyway, there wasn't much chance they would see me after school—none of *them* had to ride the bus home.

I still had my eyes focused on the toes of my tennis shoes, concentrating on getting into my little cave and out of everybody's sight, when I walked in the front door with Ellie behind me. She rode the bus, too, although she never sat with me or anything. She usually plopped herself down next to some guy.

"Hey, this is for you," she said to my back.

I just kept heading for the bedroom.

"Chey-enne," she said. You could have scraped the impatience off her voice with your finger.

"*What?*" I said.

"Do you want your mail or what?"

I turned around just as she flipped a letter out of the mail basket on the wall with her inch-long, silver fingernails.

"That's for me?"

She chomped down on her gum and gave me a you-are-so-stupid look. "No, Einstein, it's for Quasimodo. Same difference."

I snatched the envelope from her with a rude comeback already on my lips, but it faded like a puff of Avery's cigarette smoke. The letter was for me, all right, and the return address was screaming at me.

Valerie Jackson
Robinson House
1500 Center Street
Reno, NV

"A normal person would open it," Ellie said.

I didn't even think about answering her. She gave up and flounced herself, hair and all, into the kitchen. I walked like a mummy into the bedroom, still staring at the envelope.

But I didn't open it. Even after I sat on my big pillow with the thing tossed on the floor beside me, I left it sealed. I knew the minute I read it everything was going to turn to garbage.

That was what always happened when my mother was involved. I didn't even have to think about her ten seconds before the memories jammed their way into my head like little kindergarten kids saying, "Look at this one! Look at this one!"

The time she said she would take me to a storytelling, and then Julius said no and she just got drunk and went to it with him.

The time I had the only decent teacher I ever had. She said she thought she could help me do better in school, but she would have to have a conference with my mother. But my mother was too depressed the day of the meeting to come out of her room.

Or the first time Julius hit me, right across the face, and my mother just stood there and let him do it because she was too much of a wimp to stop him.

And the second time it happened.

And the third . . .

"Is it from your mother?"

Felise was standing on the other side of my curtain. Nobody else had a gruff voice that sounded as if she were calling out numbers in a football huddle.

"Yeah," I said. "Come on in."

She did, without looking at me. She hardly ever looked at anybody, which got her in trouble with drill-sergeant teachers who said she was disrespectful. She slumped her big, solid self down on my floor and pulled her naturally curly hair into a neck ponytail with the rubber band she wore on her wrist. Ellie always told her she should at least use a scrunchie because she was going to break her hair all to . . .

Well, anyway, Felise never paid attention to Ellie's beauty tips. I thought Felise was kind of cool looking anyway, especially if you could get her to smile. Then her eyes, which were this sizzly blue, would disappear. Right now she didn't smile but grunted at the letter.

"Aren't you going to open it?" she said.

"I don't want to," I said.

"Tassie will make you read it."

"I know."

"Burn it. Avery's got a lighter."

I was tempted, but I shook my head. "Ellie gave it to me.

She'll tell Tassie I got it before she can walk through the door."

"Before she can get out of her car."

Felise grunted again, and then we both sat there in silence.

"You want me to open it for you?" Felise said finally.

"Yeah," I said. "Read it out loud."

At least that way I wouldn't have to see my mother's handwriting or hear her voice in my head. Maybe I could pretend it was from somebody else.

And maybe baboons might fly out of my ears, too. The minute Felise started reading, it was like my mother was right there under the bed with us. Right from *Dear Cheyenne Summer*—the cheesy name she had given me because she was in her save-the-native-Americans phase when I was born—I wanted to rip down the curtains and punch my pillow until it threw up its stuffings.

I guess they told you I'd be writing to you, Felise read.

Yeah, they warned me.

You don't know how good it feels to finally be allowed to communicate with you.

No, you're right. I don't know. And I don't care.

I only wish it could be face to face, but this will have to do for now.

This will have to do forever, lady.

It's been so long since we've been together, I don't even know what to ask you or what to say to you. But I do want you to know that this time rehab took. I feel like a different person now and certainly a better person. When I get out of here, I'm going to have a whole different life. I think I'll be able to get a job and a decent place to live, and I promise you—

"Stop," I said.

Felise did. She gave me a quick look and then went back behind the paper.

"You don't want to hear no more?" she said.

"No," I said. "When she starts promising, I stop listening. I've heard it all before."

"I get ya," Felise said.

She folded the letter and held it out to me, but I shook my head.

"Now you can burn it," I said. "I read it, right?"

"Yeah."

"So ask Avery if you can borrow his lighter."

She left with the letter, and I did a face plant into the pillow.

Why did she have to come back out of the woodwork like that? I had all the memories shut off—I had thought for good. But just those three words, "I promise you," were enough to bring it all back, so clear, so loud, so stinking that nothing could block them out.

And believe me, I'd tried everything in the past four years.

I stayed in my cave until dinner, thinking about what I didn't want to think about. When Ellie came in and told me it was time to eat, I told her to go have her navel pierced or something. Tassie came in then and said, if I didn't get out to the table, she was going to start counting. I never let her get past "three" when she did that. I had no idea what would happen if she reached "ten," and I never wanted to find out.

"I thought we were having chili," Avery was saying as I slunk to the table and stared miserably at my plate.

"I switched to spaghetti," Tassie said.

"How come?"

"Because spaghetti is Cheyenne's favorite, and I figured she needed to have it tonight. Do you have a problem with that?"

I looked up in surprise, just in time to see Tassie giving Avery a look that said, "Say you do, and I'll have your skateboard."

Avery got it. "Guess not," he said. "Can somebody pass the cheese?"

Nobody asked me what had happened. I figured Felise had told them. She and Tassie must have threatened them, too, because nobody so much as looked at me crooked. Even Ellie, who didn't look at me at all. Some of them went out of their way to actually be decent.

Diesel said, "Cheyenne, you want some more bread?"

And from Felise it was, "I'll take your turn doin' dishes tonight."

"I'll eat your dessert for you," Avery said.

"You'll eat my shoes first," Tassie said. She didn't even raise her voice. "Besides, you and I have a date for a talk after supper."

"I'm too young to date," Avery said.

The only one who laughed was Brendan, who immediately shut up when Tassie raised her eyebrow at him.

"Talk about what?" Ellie said.

"None of your business," Avery said. His eyes started to get that close-together look.

"Why can't you fools stay out of trouble?" Ellie went on as if Avery weren't looking at her like he wished she would disintegrate.

"I'm not in trouble!"

"When I receive two phone calls from school in one day, that means trouble as I see it," Tassie said. "Now you can either talk to me, or you can talk to that vice principal I am now on a first-name basis with."

Diesel poked Avery. "I'd take the vice principal myself."

"You hush, young'un, or you and I will be havin' a date, too."

"Wouldn't that be incest?" Ellie said.

"Gross," Felise said. She pushed her cherry cobbler at me. "Eat mine, too."

In spite of how nice they were being to me, I couldn't eat hers or mine or anybody else's. My chest was pinching in so hard, it wouldn't let any food go down. I felt bad because Tassie had gone to all that trouble.

And I wasn't worth it. I was a thief with a lying, drunken mother.

When I went to bed that night, I lay there staring at the

ceiling so I wouldn't close my eyes and see my mother and Julius and my whole disgusting childhood being played out in my mind again.

I even prayed with my eyes open. *Please, God, just let me always stay here. Don't make me ever, ever go back to her.*

CHAPTER FIVE

I WAS IN ABOUT THE SAME MOOD THE NEXT DAY when somebody poked me in the back at my locker. I whirled around to give them the hairiest eyeball I could muster, and there was Tobey.

"Whoa," she said. Her brown eyes widened like a pair of Moon Pies. "Take pity. I'm unarmed."

I felt more like white trash than ever. "Sorry," I said. "I thought somebody was messing with me."

"Have you considered switching to decaf? What's up, babe?"

I turned back to my locker so she wouldn't see the guilt, which I was sure was smeared across my face. I jumbled some books around and mumbled, "Nothin'. I'm just in a bad mood."

"I hear you. I started my period this morning. I'm going to have cramps the whole weekend. I hate that."

I stood there wishing that was my biggest worry and hoping Tobey—my beloved Tobey whose very Reeboks I adored—would go away so she wouldn't see how miserable I was.

"At least it's Friday," she said. "We can all spill our guts at the Pole meeting."

Dude, it *was* Friday. We always met on Fridays at lunch to pray for each other. What was I going to say? *Would you guys please pray for me? I ripped off a shop lady the other day, and on*

*top of that my mother is starting to write me letters, and I can't
even stand to think about her. Other than that, I'm great. How are
you all?*

"Chey?" I felt Tobey's hand on my shoulder.

"Yeah?" I said, voice stiff.

"You're not going to take off on us again, are you?"

"What do you mean, 'take off'?" Of course, I knew exactly
what she was talking about. In December, when the cheating
thing went down, I'd run like a tagger in a police spotlight instead of working with the Girls. Biggest mistake I ever made.

No, make that the second biggest. My biggest mistake was
now the reason I couldn't imagine myself facing all of them
today, all of them who thought I was this unselfish little nun.

"You'll be there, right?" Tobey said.

I managed to turn around while I scrambled in my head
for an excuse not to go. But one look at her eyes, all round
and concerned, and I had to forget it. She would know the
minute I opened my mouth, and then she would tell Brianna,
and Brianna would hunt me down like bounty.

"Yeah, I'll be there," I said.

All morning long I tried to think of how to make it
through this without Brianna saying, "What is wrong with
you, girl," or Norie seeing into my head and telling Tobey or
Shannon to find out what was going on with me, or Marissa
just offering me her Doritos, which would make me bust out
crying. I was so busy with all of that, I was even less with-it
than usual in class. I flunked the vocabulary quiz in English
and read the same paragraph eight times in my special reading class and still didn't know what it said. In Spanish, *Señora*
Diaz told me she thought I was regressing. When I asked her
what that meant, she told me to go look it up. I put my head
on my desk for the rest of the hour. Even when Fletcher went
past my desk on his way to the trash can to throw away the
gum *Señora* caught him chewing and tried to cram it into my
hand, I didn't budge. Well, except to shove it back into his
and notice how warm his hands were.

Dude, I thought as I dragged myself to the theater lobby at lunchtime, *I'm usually so jazzed about the Friday meetings I make a dork out of myself. Right now I feel like I'm going to court to lie on the witness stand.*

Then, to make my day just perfect, somebody dove in front of me and said, "Hey, we have to talk about my earring!"

Fletcher again, hair still moving, smile spreading real slow across his face.

God, I thought, *please let me die. Right here. Right now.*

"Hey, Fletch." That was Norie, passing with Wyatt. "You coming to the meeting?"

"Nope," he said. "I have to make up a test in Spanish."

"Ah, *sí,*" Norie said.

I ran before Fletcher could start spewing out stuff in *español* I didn't know from trigonometry.

But at least he wasn't coming to the meeting. Maybe God did love me after all.

I wasn't any closer to a game plan, though, so I sat between Shannon and Marissa, the two who were the least likely to interrogate me under a naked light bulb, and pretended to concentrate on my lunch. Tassie had put leftover spaghetti inside a round sourdough roll and put a bread lid on it. Any other time I'd have thought I'd died and gone to heaven. But it would have taken a miracle to get me there that day.

"I brought the rest of the cake," Ms. Race sang out as she joined us. She was wearing these neat boots with South American art etched into them. Everybody squealed over those and put aside their sandwiches for cake until Tobey said, "Okay, let's get started. Who needs prayer?"

There were a couple of requests—I wasn't really listening, which was why Shannon had to nudge me.

"What?" I said.

"Do you need prayer for anything this week?" she said.

"Did you take a little trip off to Aruba or something, Chey?" Norie said.

I shook my head. Ms. Race leaned back on her hands and looked at me across the circle. "That wasn't the answer I expected," she said.

"I thought you'd say, 'Where's Aruba?'" Brianna said. She looked blankly at Norie. "Where *is* Aruba?"

Normally I would have asked that. I wasn't very good at this disguising-your-feelings thing.

"You really look down, Cheyenne," Ms. Race said. "Why don't you let us pray for you?"

"I'm okay," I said.

Norie made a loud buzzing noise. "That is an incorrect answer," she said.

Marissa touched my arm. "Whatever it is, you know you can trust us. We're not going to say it's stupid or anything."

"Right!" Tobey said. "If you guys can pray that my zit will disappear before the speech contest, nothing is too stupid!"

"Talk, girl," Brianna said.

Shannon pressed against me from the other side and said, "It's okay."

I was almost tempted to bawl or worse, confess. I said the only thing I could think of to get them to stop looking at me like I was even worth caring about. "Y'know, we pray for each other all the time. But, I mean, really, do any of our prayers get answered?"

"Good question!" Ms. Race said. She sat up straight and hugged her knees, which were clad in these long, wool, wide-legged pants. "Can anybody say yes to that?"

"I definitely can," Norie said. "And so can Tobey. You know that, Cheyenne."

"I have. I mean, it isn't a big thing like theirs." Marissa shrugged and folded and unfolded her Doritos bag. "Last week we prayed for me not to be so shy, and when Jerry Pavella asked me out, I didn't, like, look at the floor and say yes because I was too scared to say no."

"I hope you punched him out," Norie said.

Marissa gave her soft little laugh. "I just looked at him and said, 'I don't think so.'" She squeezed her eyes shut. "Then I ran!"

"That's big though," Tobey said. "And I totally think it was prayer that helped you—I mean, don't you?"

"Definitely."

Beside me, Shannon sighed. "I'm still waiting," she said. "You know, for my big prayer to be answered about my sister. But I'm not giving up, Cheyenne. Look at Tobey. It took months before people really started being nice to her again. Maybe it just takes time."

"Bottom line is," Norie said crisply, "you have to ask."

"Then God can start dealing with you," Ms. Race said.

"Oh, I got one," Brianna said. "This is going to blow you away . . ."

She went off about something. I didn't even get the first sentence. My mind was headed in a different direction.

Why isn't God answering any of my prayers then? I was thinking. It took me all of about two seconds to figure that one out.

Because you messed up so bad, I answered myself. *You can't go around swiping stuff and then expect God to come to your rescue.*

That was it, of course. I could feel it in the pinching twist of guilt in my chest. I didn't really have to steal those beads. Brianna had said it: The Girls just wanted me; it wouldn't have mattered if I hadn't given her a present. But now God was dealing with me. He was sicking my mother on me.

I forced myself to focus on the group. They were all laughing about something Brianna had just said. I laughed, too, although I didn't have a clue why. Brianna nudged my foot with hers.

"That's more like it, girl," she said. "Don't you go hiding

your face and running off. We've already been there. You hear what I'm saying?"

"Yeah," I said. I gave the plastic smile, and then we held hands and prayed. Then the bell rang.

I took my time throwing away my trash so everybody would leave except Ms. Race. She didn't even look surprised when I said, "Can I talk to you?"

She gave me her wrinkled-nose smile and pulled a pad of hall passes out of her pocket. "Take as long as you want," she said.

I wrung the straps of my backpack. She held the passes and waited.

Forget it, I thought. *This is stupid. As soon as I say this, she's going to want to know why I'm asking, and then she'll pry it out of me, and then it'll be all over.*

But it already felt "all over." I hadn't been any more a part of that circle at lunch than one of those stupid little taggers in the lobby jeering "Jesus freak!" I'd spent most of my life feeling lonely, but right now was the loneliest I'd ever been.

I guess that's why I had to know, and why the words rushed out of me headlong. "Does God stop answering your prayers if you turn into a dirty, awful person?" I said.

I waited for the torrent of questions. Ms. Race didn't even blink. She looked like she was thinking hard about that—and that gave me a speck of hope. If there was no set answer, maybe it wasn't just "yes."

Finally she pushed her braid over her shoulder and gave me a little nod, like she was okay with what she was about to say. "I figure I'm clean," she said.

I'm not! I thought.

"But it isn't because I've never done anything wrong," she went on. "It's because I've been washed."

I didn't get it for a second. She looked like she was waiting for me to.

"You mean, like you were baptized?" I said.

"That's the symbolic part," she said. "But I have to be washed by the Lord, oh, about twenty times a day."

"No way," I said. "You don't mess up that much!"

"Of course I do," she said. "I'm a person."

I still shook my head. "I'd believe that about that kid over there," I said. I pointed to a guy with his boxers showing above his jeans waist. Even as we watched him he slammed his hand against the side of the pay phone and looked at Ms. Race to see if she was going to do anything about it. "But I wouldn't believe it about you," I said.

"The biggest difference between him and me," Ms. Race said when he was gone, "is that I ask God to forgive me when I do something stupid." Her crinkly blue eyes twinkled. "I'm pretty sure that kid doesn't."

"What if he did?" I said. "That kid's been in so much trouble, God would probably tell him to get lost."

I wasn't sure whether I was talking about the tagger or myself. I bit my lip so I'd shut up.

Ms. Race did something surprising then. She reached out and brushed my hair back from my face on both sides. Nobody had done that for me since—well, maybe never. My chest pinched hard.

"Actually, Cheyenne," she said, "I think God gets the biggest kick out of the toughest cases. When somebody like that comes to Him and asks to have all his garbage wiped away so he can live a different life, I think God loves that. How could He show how loving He was if He only forgave little things? Anybody can do that. It takes a lot to forgive a lifetime of big mistakes."

"Does He do it?" I said.

"All you have to do is ask," she said.

I didn't say anything. It was a concept I didn't have a whole lot of experience with. I liked it, but I wasn't sure I believed it yet.

Ms. Race pulled out the passes again. "Are you ready for this?" she said.

"Yeah," I said, "But could you make it for like five minutes from now?"

"Sure," she said. She didn't look at me as she wrote, but when she handed me the pass, her eyes locked right on mine. "There's a bench right around that corner," she said. "Nobody will bother you there for a few minutes."

With another crinkly smile, she touched my arm and walked away. I stood there until the sound of her boot heels disappeared behind the double doors, and then I found the bench.

She knew I was going to sit right down and try it, I thought.

Anybody who knew me for more than an hour could have figured that out. But what else *was* there to do? It had to be better than the torture I was going through.

As I sat on the bench and put my face in my hands, I found myself brushing my hair back the way Ms. Race had done. I closed my eyes and tried hard to think what to say. There weren't too many ways to put it.

God? I took those beads for Brianna's present. I thought I had to have them. I thought I'd be, like, a total outcast if I didn't give her something. But now I feel more like an outsider than ever. Will you forgive me? Am I okay now?

I waited, holding my breath. I guess I kind of expected an answer right away. It would have been nice if a vision of an angel had appeared in front of me, assuring me that I was now officially clean and could get on with my life.

Maybe there would have been a peaceful feeling. I don't know. I never had a chance to find out. Even as I sat there, eyes closed, I suddenly felt like a little girl again. The eight-year-old who had just told her mother she had broken the lamp.

Then there she was, the mother with the baggy, red eyes and mouth ready to rip open and tear me apart with her words: *Why do you do things like that, Cheyenne? Are you stupid? How many times do I have to tell you to watch what you're doing?*

Save your breath, another voice said. It slammed its way into my thoughts the way Julius always did, jagged and cruel and too loud to shout over. *There's only one way to make her remember. Get over here, Cheyenne!*

"Cheyenne!"

It took me several slams of my heart to realize it wasn't Julius calling me.

It was Fletcher.

He was standing over the bench with his smile only about halfway there. I bolted up so he wouldn't think I was some kind of weirdo and stomped down right on his foot. He looked at it and started to yelp like a dog.

"Shhh," I hissed. "We'll get in trouble!"

He stopped the puppy routine and shook his head, setting his foot back down, miraculously cured. "I'm in drama class," he said. "Mr. Pratt lets us come out here to rehearse. He'll think it's part of our scene or something." He nodded across the lobby. "My group's over there."

"Oh," I said.

"What are you doing here?" he said. "I thought you were in a coma or something. I was about to call 911." He grinned. "I guess I could have tried CPR."

I giggled, of course.

"I was just thinking," I said.

Then I cringed and waited for it. The "Oh, you mean you actually *think*? Didn't recognize the expression on your face. I thought I smelled something burning!"

But Fletcher finished getting the smile on his face and said, "Think about this, okay? My dad won't let me have my ear pierced. Big surprise, right?"

I got out a "Bummer."

"Yeah, well, I bet Tobey five bucks he would so now I'm broke, too."

I hear ya, I thought.

"So forget making me an earring. But you know what would be cool?"

"No," I said.

"You could make me, like, a friendship bracelet."

I know I looked as if I were retarded, standing there with my mouth hanging open. Any minute drool was going to appear. But I was stunned. Fletcher L'Orange wanted me to make him a friendship bracelet?

Yeah, right was my next thought. *For him to give Shannon or what's her name, Victoria, or some other little chickie.*

I shrugged and tried not to look like I was crushed about as low as I was going to get in one day.

"Does that mean 'yes'?" he said.

"Sure," I said. "What color does she want?"

"Who?" Fletcher said. He swished back his hair. "It's for me. I'm going to wear it." The grin started up again. "I'm going to call it an amino bracelet."

"Dude," I said, "don't you ever cut anybody any slack?"

"Nah. Well, not you, anyway."

"Why me?" I said. I couldn't help it. I was starting to grin, myself. Who would have thought I'd ever smile again?

"'Cause you get all red in the face when I mess with your head," he said. "It's cute."

Cute. Fletcher L'Orange had just called me cute. Once again I was struck dumb.

"See, you're doing it right now!" he said. Before I could even grasp what he was doing, he put both hands on my face and looked into it. I'd have folded right there if somebody hadn't squealed from across the lobby, "Fletcher, Mr. Pratt's going to come out here and bust us if you don't get over here!"

Fletcher dropped his hands from my face and started to back up, still grinning. "If I get one more detention, my dad's going to ground me till I'm dead," he said. "Remember, I like purple."

"Okay," I said. I didn't move.

"Don't you have to go to class?" he said.

I held up my hall pass and stared at it stupidly. "Oh yeah," I said.

But getting there was the last thing on my mind, even as I hurried off to the double doors.

Nah, I was thinking about one thing, and that was getting back to the bead store.

Whatever I had to do, I was going to make an amino bracelet for Fletcher.

CHAPTER SIX

I SOMETIMES LIKE TO TELL MYSELF THAT IF I HAD had just one hint that God had forgiven me, I wouldn't have done what I did that afternoon. But the truth is I wasn't even thinking about God. I was only thinking about a plan, and it unfolded like a piece of silk. Make that fake silk.

When I got home from school, Diesel was having a "discussion" with Tassie. "It's only going to take me half an hour," he was saying to her in the kitchen.

"You've never spent less than an hour and a half in an auto-parts store in your life, Dennis McBrien," Tassie said.

Felise gave a grunt from one of the love seats in the living room. "I didn't know his real name was 'Dennis,'" she whispered to me.

"Look, you can time me, Ma," Diesel said. "I'll just go, get the stuff, and come right back. Then I'll shovel the whole thing."

"You better believe you will, and Mrs. Chang's, too. If you wait till the sun goes down, that whole sidewalk is going to turn to ice again, and we'll have people breaking their necks all over the place."

"Hopefully that would include Avery and Brendan," I heard Ellie comment from somewhere in the vicinity of the refrigerator. She had announced that morning that she had PMS. She was probably looking for chocolate.

parseFloat

"All right," Tassie said. "Grand Auto and then right back here. I'll have the shovel waitin' for you."

I chuckled to myself. Grand Theft Auto, Ms. Race had called it.

Then I froze. Hadn't she said that when she was giving us directions to the shops?

This had to be some kind of fate thing. I grabbed Diesel as he sailed out of the kitchen.

"Can I go with you?" I said.

"You want to go to the auto-parts store?" he said. His face was blank, except for some kind of greasy stuff that was smeared down his cheek.

"I want to go across the street from there. Can I go?" I tried to beguile him with a grin. "I promise I won't talk much."

"Yeah right," Ellie called out from the kitchen.

"You go on with him, Cheyenne," Tassie said. Her eyes were sparkling. "I'm makin' you responsible for seeing that he's back here by three-thirty and not one minute later."

"I can do that," I said. "I'll put him in a headlock or something. Well, maybe not that. I'd probably break my arm, but I'll get him back here. Don't even worry about it."

I was halfway out the door. Diesel just shrugged. He didn't care, as long as he could get his hands on all those carburetors and overhead cams, whatever they were.

I really didn't do my usual jaw-jacking on the way to Plumb Lane. I was too busy convincing myself that, if I made a bracelet for Fletcher and we started to go out, that was going to make up for a lot of other things I was never going to have.

"Meet me here by three-twenty," Diesel said as he pulled into Grand Auto and jammed the truck into park. "Or Ma's going to have a cow."

"And you'll be grounded till you're dead," I said.

That sounded so clever. Of course, Fletcher had said it. Fletcher L'Orange, who thought I was cute.

I guess that just took over somehow as I made my way across the icy highway to the bead shop. I was inside before I even thought about Angel Lady. That's when the next part slid into place: She wasn't there.

I wandered around the whole shop looking for her, but the only other person was a guy sitting behind the counter reading a newspaper, as if he were baby-sitting the place and wasn't too happy about it.

A sort of tingly feeling came over me. It convinced me that this was going to be a snap.

I gave him one more look from over the leather display, and then I headed for the beads. I wish I could say that for a minute my chest pinched and I wondered if I should really be doing this. I definitely wish I'd given God, the Flagpole Girls, and even my "family" a second thought.

But I'm not sure I did. I only know I gazed at those beads thinking one thing: *Fletcher likes purple.*

The bracelet was going to have to be a masculine-looking piece, of course. I'd figured all that out on the bus. There were some big, heavy-looking beads in a dark, woodsy purple—amethyst globes—that I could connect with a leather strip. Two of these. Three of these. This wasn't half what I'd lifted for Brianna. They wouldn't even miss them. And I had to have them.

And I did. They were in my hand, suddenly dull against the sparkles of sweat in my palm. I think I really did get a pinch in my chest then, a knot that made me whisper to myself, *Wait a minute.*

I closed my fingers over the beads. Then I opened them. My hand moved back to the bins they had come from—and then I pulled my hand toward my pocket.

The door jangled and a springy voice said, "How did it go?"

It was Angel Lady. Whether her sitter answered or not, I don't know. I convulsed like I was having a seizure. Beads went everywhere.

"What's happening over here?" Angel Lady said.

I lurched toward the floor where I could see a solitary purple bead rolling toward her feet. But I froze in mid-pose and screeched at myself, *Pick them up! No, run! Run like a mad dog! Don't be stupid! It's over! Confess! Tell her you're a dirty little thief!*

But I didn't have to say anything. Angel Lady squatted right down and scooped up the bead. She looked at it as reverently as I had.

"I'm so sorry," she said. "I bet you had these all picked out for something. Did I startle you?"

"You could say that," I said.

I didn't even recognize my own voice. I sounded like a terminally ill person about to go the way of all flesh.

"Well, let's get them picked up. I'm sure you remember what you had, and whatever we don't find on the floor, there's more in the bins."

On hands and creaky old knees she chatted cheerfully while picking up the beads. I retrieved one. I couldn't move much beyond that. My whole body was seized up with one question, *How am I going to get out of this?*

"I have four," she said, holding on to a shelf to get to her feet. "Did you find the rest?"

I nodded numbly and handed the bead over.

"All right!" Her voice was sweet and pure as she more or less floated toward the counter. "Anything else for you?"

No! I wanted to scream. *I don't even want that!*

But to my horror, she spread the precious beads on a piece of velvet and turned to the cash register. The guy behind the newspaper glanced up, gave my booty a disapproving look, and scowled back at the page. I had a clear vision of his being the one to tie my hands behind my back while they waited for the police.

Run! I shouted in my head. *Run now!*

Right. With Mr. *Reno Gazette-Journal* on my tail. This couldn't be worse.

Then suddenly it was. Angel Lady stopped in the middle of putting the register through its beeps and smiled at me. There were angels in her eyes, too.

"What are you going to make, dear?" she said.

"What?" I said.

"From the beads. What are you making?"

"Oh," I said. I was still talking in my cancer-patient voice. "A friendship bracelet."

"Well," she said. "I'm so glad you found something. I remember you left disappointed last time."

This went beyond horror. The woman remembered me. There was something so crushing about that I could hardly breathe. I had to get out of there, or I was sure I was going to suffocate.

I stole a glance at the glass door, looking for an escape route. There might as well have been a sea of crocodiles for all the good it was going to do me. Because there, on the other side of the door, was Diesel. He was peering in. Looking for me.

My mind went on fast forward. He couldn't find me in here, standing at the counter while this lady was ringing up the sale. He knew I didn't have any money. He would be in here so fast asking questions, and then I'd be the one grounded until I was dead.

In Wittenberg.

And I would rather be dead than go back there.

I shoved away from the counter and flung myself at the door. It all happened so fast, and yet it was as if the whole thing happened in slow-mo.

I could feel her kind eyes on my back. I could hear her voice, calling, gently, to me, "Is there something wrong, dear?"

I was all the way to the end of the sidewalk when Diesel caught up with me. He lowered his forehead at me.

"Where have you been?" he said, his voice a growl. "We have five minutes to get home now!"

Diesel could be pretty scary. If his hands hadn't been wedged into the pockets of his skintight jeans, I'd have been worried he was going to pick me up by the back of my flannel and haul me bodily to the truck.

But all I was really worried about right then was whether he had seen me standing at that counter like I was about to make a major purchase.

Please, God, I prayed, *make it so he didn't see me. Make it so she won't come after me—or that guy.*

I didn't dare glance over my shoulder. Nobody grabbed me from behind or yelled, "Freeze!" But even after we climbed into the truck, I kept my eyes squeezed shut, and I kept praying.

Fine time to think about God, huh?

He still wasn't the major thing on my mind. All through dinner, homework, even when I was buried in my cave, all I could think of or see or hear was Angel Lady. She was so nice. She was so good she didn't even suspect I'd been about to rip her off when she came in and found me with beads all over her shop floor. I didn't even think about Fletcher or how I was going to make his bracelet now. And I didn't count myself lucky that at least I hadn't gotten in trouble. It was weird. But all I could think about was her.

And how lousy I now felt about Cheyenne Summer Jackson.

I didn't come out of my cave all evening, even when Tassie came by and said, "Prayer time if anybody's interested."

A lot of times I was. Those were cool times to hang out with Tassie and Diesel. Tonight I pulled back my curtain and said, "No thanks. I'm going to bed."

Felise looked up at me from her sketchbook and grunted. That meant she wanted to talk. She had probably been waiting for me to come out all night.

"That black chick is in my art class," she said.

"Brianna?" I said.

"Yeah." Felise sketched for another half a minute, and

then she grunted again. "She had on these cool earrings today. I told her I liked them."

Something about this conversation was starting to make me uneasy. I didn't answer.

"She said you made them for her," Felise went on. "Those were nice beads. How did you pull that off anyway?"

"Huh," somebody else said.

I about jumped a foot. Ellie was up in her bed, doing her nails. Miss I've-got-to-get-the-dirt-on-everybody-so-I-can-get-them-in-trouble must have slipped in earlier without my hearing her.

"You actually have taste?" she said to me.

At times like that I wished a topic fairy would come down and magically change the subject. There was no other way to get out of this.

"At least I don't wear silver nail polish," I said.

"On what?" Ellie said. "You have stubs for fingernails. Tassie doesn't feed you enough, you have to eat your body parts?"

"Gross!" I said.

Ellie went on about the rest of my scraggly-looking appearance, and I breathed a sigh of relief. But through it all, Felise was still sketching and still grunting. Once she even looked up at me. She knew exactly what I was doing.

I was getting more scared by the minute. And I didn't even know the half of it.

The next day, Saturday, we were all doing our assigned house chores when Brianna called me. Usually Tassie didn't let us take phone calls until we were done, but "since it's her," Tassie gave me the phone to the tune of Ellie wailing, "That is so unfair!"

"Hey, girl," Brianna said. Her voice was always so rich and calm. Dude, I really loved her. Just then, that fact made me incredibly sad.

"Hi," I said.

"What are you doing today?"

"Nothing," I said.

Big mistake. I left myself wide open.

"You want to hang with me?" she said. "Everybody's been saying how much they love the earrings you made for me, so I'm thinking I want to learn how to make them. If I drive you over to that bead store, will you help me pick out the stuff?"

"The bead store?" I said stupidly. "You mean, the one where I got yours?"

"Yeah," she said. She hesitated. "What, are they way expensive or something?"

"I don't know," I said.

"What do you mean you don't know? You just bought stuff there. You don't have to tell me how much they cost, but I have ten dollars. Will that cover it?"

"I don't know," I said again. "But I can't go today." I was floundering helplessly, but I just latched on the first excuse I could think of. "I have to do a bunch of homework," I said. "Boy, they can sure load it on for the weekends. You would think we were in college—"

"You're going to do homework on Saturday?"

"Yeah, I want to get ahead."

There was this long silence. She might as well have screamed, "I do not believe you!"

"All right," she said finally. "Put Diesel on, would you? Ira wants to talk to him."

I handed the phone to Diesel, with Ellie still squawking about equal rights, and went back to my rag and can of Pledge.

I'm so far out of their league I can't even make up a classy lie, I thought miserably.

When I finished polishing, I checked the chore off the list and headed for my room. Tassie had other ideas.

"Oh no you don't, young'un," she said before I even got to the door.

"What?" I said.

"You are not going to hole up in that room again today. You're turning into a hermit, and I'm not havin' it."

"But—"

"You put on your coat and walk down to the 7-Eleven to buy me a newspaper. I want to see what's playing at the movies."

"Can't Ellie go?"

"No, Ellie cannot go," said Ellie. "I have a date this afternoon."

Tassie stared her down. "If I think this boy is decent when he comes to pick you up."

"And if the dude doesn't hurl when he sees you," Avery put in.

Ellie rolled her eyes and went back to mopping the kitchen floor.

"Go on, put on your coat," Tassie said to me. Then she folded her arms across her massive chest and just looked.

There was no getting out of it. I shrugged into the hated mended down jacket, poked my hands into its pockets, and trudged off toward Seventh Street.

It was the kind of Nevada winter day I usually found pretty awesome. There was fresh snow, not yucked over from the cars yet, and the sky was streaked with feathery cloud formations that reminded me of snowy white Indian jewelry.

But I directed my face toward the sidewalk and just plowed toward the 7-Eleven. Nothing was pretty about the day, as far as I was concerned, and nothing was pretty about my thoughts. They went in ugly circles strung together:

I will never be as good as the rest of the Girls. I don't even think like them.

I might as well forget about being friends with them anymore—if I ever was.

I might as well forget about ever feeling clean like Ms. Race said. God's obviously ignoring my prayers—when I pray them.

And who could blame Him? I'm a loser. That's just who I am.

That's who Julius told me I was, and my mother agreed with him. They must have been right.

The last time through, though, something added itself on, like a bump in the circle. *God, please don't let them be right. Just once let me be right.*

That may have been the only thing that kept me from stepping right out into Seventh Street in the path of some oncoming car and ending it all.

As it was, a car pulled up beside me, a pickup truck from the sound of it. I didn't look up at it, not until somebody got out of it and grabbed me from behind.

"Hey!" I yelled.

"Just get in the truck," a gruff voice said. "We're goin' for a ride."

"DIESEL, YOU ABOUT SCARED ME TO DEATH!" I screamed at him. "Let me out; it smells in here!"

But he just kept driving up Seventh Street. On the other side of me, Felise was sitting there like she was taking a routine run to Safeway.

"What's going on?" I said.

Diesel didn't answer. Felise grunted, of course, and flipped her ponytail to one side. "Like he said, we're takin' you for a ride," she said.

"No duh!" I said. "Did you have to assault me? I could press charges for something like this."

"You watch too much TV," Diesel said. "This isn't an assault. It's a kidnapping."

He turned on the blinker and took the corner at McCarran Boulevard.

"Where are we going?" I said. "What if I don't want to go?"

"Like you got a choice," Diesel said.

I looked at Felise, but she was calmly gazing out the window. She must have breathed too much transmission fluid, because something strange was going on here, and she was acting like we were off to a picnic.

"Come on, you guys. What are we doing?"

Diesel turned onto Mae Anne Drive, and I groaned. "We're not going to the school, are we?"

Felise gave a loud grunt, even for her. "No way. I don't go near that place unless I have to."

"Well, what else is up here?" I said.

Diesel just pointed through the windshield at the mountains, which were now huge mounds of snow with the occasional piñon pine poking out.

"We're going up there?" I said.

He patted his dashboard. "She's got four-wheel drive."

That was all he would say, no matter how much I whined and badgered. Felise, naturally, was useless.

"I'm not kidding," I said. "I could bring a lawsuit. You would both be in juvie so fast. You'll be worse than grounded, Diesel, especially if anything happens to me. You're almost eighteen. They could try you in adult court; you could end up in Carson City. Have you ever been to that prison? I have. My mother made me go there to visit Julius one time when she thought they were going to get back together after he was 'rehabilitated.' You don't get rehabilitated there. You just get grosser and more stupid."

"Take a breath, would ya?" Diesel said.

He shifted down to second and pulled the truck off the pavement and onto a dirt road that as far as I could see went straight up. The truck clanked and groaned, and Diesel shifted down one more time. I grabbed the dash with one hand and Felise's leg with the other.

"We're going to be killed!"

"You are, if you don't shut up," Diesel said.

"No dessert for you tonight," Felise muttered to him.

Clearly they weren't going to be put off from what was turning out to be a pretty scary trip. I clung with my fingernails, such as they were, while Diesel ground the gears and took us over the peaks of hills and down ninety degrees into valleys and back up mountains like Spiderman.

By about the fifth incline, it started to feel like a roller coaster. I'd only been on one. Julius was going through a brief, I-am-a-wonderful-father stage and took us to Great America in California. I liked roller coasters.

I caught myself almost laughing. "We're not going to die?" I said.

"Do I look dead?" Diesel opened the window a crack and spat for effect. "I do this all the time."

"In the snow?" I said.

"That's when it's the most fun."

To prove it, he yanked the wheel to the right, and we started to spin. I squealed, and even Felise grabbed the seat and grinned. Her eyes disappeared, and so did some of my ticked-offness. By the time Diesel pulled the truck to a stop at the top of one of the tallest of the mountains, I was laughing out loud.

Then I stopped and gasped like I was two years old and seeing my first string of Christmas lights.

"Dude," I said.

"Yeah," Diesel said.

He was looking pretty smug, and he had a right to. He had just pulled us up to the most incredible view I had ever seen. Below us, all of Reno was scattered like a toy town trying to wriggle its way out from under a white blanket. Above us, the sky was already tinged with a late afternoon red glow that wisped across the mountain snow here and there, too. It was really like being on top of the world.

"Dude," I said again. "This is beautiful."

The feeling lasted about five minutes, and then reality crashed back in. "You would be in so much trouble if Tassie knew you came up here," I said.

"Why?" Diesel said. "I've brought her up here a couple of times."

"No way."

"She thinks it's cool. She says you're closer to God up here or somethin'. Figures she would come up with something religious."

My chest pinched in. *I wish she was right,* I thought. But the point was, of course, that God probably didn't want to be close to me. I had some nerve even coming up here like I could be closer to God.

I turned to Diesel. "So why did you bring me?" I said.

He glanced at Felise. "Insurance," he said.

"Insurance? What do I know from insurance? I'm four-teen!"

"The insurance was for us," Felise said. "We figured if we couldn't get it out of you, we'd just threaten to leave you up here."

"Threaten?" Diesel said. "I'd do it, no lie."

"Get what out of me?" I said. This was becoming less like a winter wonderland and more like a trap. I started to squirm.

Diesel jolted the seat back so he could sling his leg up over the steering wheel. He took a toothpick out of his pocket and poked at his gums with it for a second. Then he lowered his eyebrows at me.

"You're in some kind of trouble," he said.

"I am not."

"You couldn't lie your way out of a plastic bag," Felise said. "You would suffocate first."

I'm suffocating now, I thought.

"You can't deny it," Diesel said. "You've been walkin' around lookin' guilty for days."

"And hidin' under your bed," Felise said. "Tassie thinks you're going into a depression. She's about to haul you off to the doctor."

"I am depressed," I said. "I have every right to be. My mother is starting to write to me . . ."

It didn't work. They just looked at me, even Felise. I stuttered to a stop and started to bite my fingernails.

"Tell us what you did," Diesel said. "It can't be worse than anything else I ever heard. We live with Avery and Brendan, remember?"

Felise grunted. "And Ellie."

"I can't tell you," I said. "If I do, I'll end up in Wittenberg again. I might as well kill myself!"

"Shut up!"

I looked up at Felise. She definitely didn't care about dessert. Her eyes were blazing blue.

"You don't say stuff like that!" she said. "Or pretty soon you start believin' it, and then you're doin' it. So just shut up!"

In a twisted kind of way, I felt loved. The same way I'd felt the day Brianna pulled me into Ira's truck and told me to get straight because they expected it of me.

I bit my lip, but it didn't help. I started to cry. I could feel Diesel tightening up beside me. Evidently, he didn't like it when people cried.

"There's nothin' we ain't either seen or heard of or done ourselves," Felise said. "But if you keep it locked up, you're going to do worse. That's about the only thing I learned from that shrink they sent me to. I'm the biggest lockjaw of them all, but I wouldn't keep something like this from you guys. I'd be spillin' it in a minute."

And I would be there for her, I knew that. Just like I'd been for Norie and for Tobey. Like I'd tried to be for my mother.

And Felise was better than me. She'd be there . . .

I let go of my lip and let the tears come. It wasn't pretty, but somehow I bawled my way through it.

"I stole those beads for Brianna's earrings," I said. "I thought I had to. I thought I'd be the biggest geek if I didn't have a present. I'm enough of a dork with the Girls as it is. And then I found out they didn't care about that, so I felt like this big loser. I mean, I can't even pray anymore because God hates me now. I'm not clean. I'm this dirty, little, lying, stupid thief! And I thought if I could just have Fletcher it might be all right. I could forget about the stealing or something. Only he wanted me to make him this bracelet, so I was going to steal again, and I would have but the lady almost caught me, and then Diesel came, and I freaked out and ran. Only no-body will let it go. Brianna wants me to go back there, but I can't! I'm so scared!"

I plastered my hands over my face and just sobbed. Nobody said anything. Once I felt a hand go across my back, and I was pretty sure it wasn't Felise's. I cried until I was done because nobody stopped me. It was kind of a gift, you know? I felt about an inch better just dumping it.

But when I lifted my head, I knew right away they didn't feel better. Diesel was studying the fading sky, and Felise was popping the rubber band she had taken off her ponytail.

"I'm sorry, you guys," I said.

"*You're* sorry?" Diesel said. "I feel like a useless sack of cow manure. I don't know what to do about this."

Felise grunted. She didn't either.

"You don't have to do anything," I said miserably. "It's my problem."

"No way!" Diesel's eyes flashed. "We wanted to help you; now we're going to help you. It's just hard, that's all."

"Hard?" I said. "It's impossible. I'm probably not even—"

I stopped. I'd been about to say "worth it," but I knew what kind of flak I'd get from both sides. Besides, if they had dragged me all the way up here, and they were this bummed out because they didn't have any answers for me, I must be worth *something*.

"Okay, look," Felise said finally. She had talked more that afternoon than during the whole time I'd known her. "Probably nobody is ever going to find out. You could just make a vow never to do it again, and we'd help you. Alcoholics have sponsors; we could be your steal-o-holic sponsors."

Diesel sniffed. "I don't think that's going to work," he said.

"Why?"

"'Cause. First off, if anybody ever finds out you knew, Felise, you would be in trouble, too, and you can't afford it any more than she can."

"I've messed everything up!" I wailed. "Now even you're busted!"

"Would you shut up, Cheyenne?" Diesel said. "Man, you got the both of you locked up for twenty years, and you haven't even been caught yet. Just chill a minute. You drive me nuts."

He might as well have said, "I love you." I sank back into the seat.

"Besides," he went on, "like you said, nobody will leave it alone. This is going to sound weird, okay, but I think God wants it to come out, so it's going to come out. I figure it's better for it to come from you than for somebody to expose you or somethin'."

I gaped at him. "You mean like . . . confess?"

"I don't know. Maybe. And I'm thinkin' the ones to really help you with this are Tobey and Brianna, all them."

I shook my head so hard I could almost feel my brain sloshing around. "No way," I said, teeth gritted. "They can't know. They would never speak to me again if they found out I was some kind of klepto. I mean it, Diesel, we can't tell them."

Diesel looked over my head at Felise, and I could have sworn I saw a smile start to twitch at the corners of his mouth.

"What?" I said. "What's so funny? This isn't a joke, Diesel. I am so serious. You are not telling them!"

I heard Felise grunt. Diesel wiped his mouth with his hand.

"I don't have to tell them," he said.

I shot up in the seat. "What do you mean? You already did?"

"Nope," he said. He looked at me from under his forehead-hood. "They're the ones who put *me* wise, Cheyenne. They already know."

CHAPTER EIGHT

I MUST HAVE STARED AT HIM FOR A GOOD MINUTE. The first words that came out of my mouth were: "You're lying."

"No, that's *your* M.O.," he said. "Why would I lie about something like that?"

"How do they know then?" I said.

"Think about it," Felise said. "You have holes in your tennis shoes, but you come up with these expensive-looking earrings for somebody's birthday? Then you tell Brianna you can't go out with her because you have to do homework—on a Saturday?"

"Besides," Diesel said, "those girls are like psychic or something. Brianna said she just had this feeling, and she said Tobey did, too. They know you, Cheyenne. Probably better than we do."

Just then that fact wasn't very comforting. I wanted to die.

"I don't know what your problem is," Felise said. "If I had a bunch of friends who cared about me as much as they do about you, I'd be at one of their houses so fast. Shoot, after facin' down sexual assault and being framed for possession of marijuana, what's a little shoplifting to them?"

"A *little* shoplifting?" I said. "Tobey and Norie didn't break the law. I did!"

"So go to them," Diesel said. "Have one of those powwow things and just dump it. They'll think of something."

"I don't know," I said miserably.

"I do," Felise said. "If you don't tell 'em, I will."

It looked like I didn't have a choice. The only say I had in it was *when*. I got Diesel and Felise to give me until Monday. I needed a day to figure out how I was going to do it. Maybe I'd tell Norie when she came over to tutor me Sunday afternoon, and then she could break it to everybody else.

I guess God really did care about me after all. Norie called up sounding like a frog and said she was sick and couldn't make it for the tutoring.

After that, no matter how hard I tried to figure out an easy way to do it, only one thing would come to me. Along with visions of being hauled off to Wittenberg again. Or having my mother shaking her head and saying, "I knew you were hopeless. Julius and I told you that."

Sunday night I crawled into my cave—Tassie finally gave me permission to hole up—and I wrote a note.

> *Dear Tobey,*
> *I'm in trouble. Big surprise, huh? I don't expect you guys to get me out of it or anything, but maybe you could help me think of the right thing to do. I haven't been able to think of anything right lately. Can we please meet at lunch? Could you set it up? Could you help me not to chicken out?*
>
> > *Cheyenne*

I slept like a baby that night. I guess because I'd done the first sensible thing since . . . well, maybe ever.

The next morning Diesel drove me to school, me and Felise. They walked on either side of me like a pair of bookends to Tobey's locker and watched me shove the note in through the little vents.

"You're doing the right thing," Diesel told me. His face turned stern. "Now look, if you start feelin' like you want to

ditch this or somethin', you come down to auto shop, and I'll
set you straight."

Felise looked up at the clock. "I can't help you after seven-
thirty. I'll be in detention all day."

"For what?" I said.

"I wouldn't answer Mr. Hopkins when he asked me a question."

"How come you didn't?" I said.

"Because it was an insulting question," she said. "I wasn't
going to give him the satisfaction."

"Wow," I said.

But as I went off to English, I secretly wished that was the
biggest problem I had. I was pretty sure nobody could insult
me. I was so far down, anything they said would probably be
the truth.

I brightened up a little bit, though, when Brianna found
me in the hall after third period and got me in a headlock
next to the water fountain. "Are you all right, girl?" she said.

Ira stood in front of us, suspiciously glancing over his big
shoulders at the hall mob.

"Somebody giving you a bad time?" he said. "You know all
you have to do is say something, and I'll take care of it—
Diesel and me."

"It isn't anything like that," I said. It was kind of hard to
talk. I was verging on crying again. I had this dread-feeling, like
they were being so sweet, and yet it might be the last time they
would ever speak to me after what they were about to find out.

"Okay," Brianna said, "long as you're safe. We'll see you at
the meeting."

I suddenly had a horrible thought. "Are you coming to the
meeting, Ira?" I said.

"Unless you don't want me there," he said.

I shook my head violently. "What I want you to do is keep
Fletcher from coming. He can't know about this. Please."

Ira didn't even flick an eyelash. "Done," he said. "I'll get

Wyatt and Diesel to help me. We'll tell Fletcher no guys allowed."

Brianna gave me a tight hug, and I was good to go.

Lunchtime came all too quickly, and I was surrounded by eyes brimming with concern and hands that wanted to hug me, pat me, and stroke my hair. I felt so loved and so worthless at the same time it was about to tear me apart. Diesel had been right; I did want to ditch this whole thing. I even glanced at the exit sign.

But Ms. Race caught my arm, mind reader that she was, and said, "Why don't we sit down and get started?"

I gave one more look around, just to be sure Fletcher wasn't lurking someplace, but I saw no sign of him. Somehow, Ms. Race had even managed to eliminate all the skater kids. It was just the Girls and me.

"I have this feeling," Tobey said, "that I should start off with a prayer. Anybody mind?"

"Go, girl," Brianna said.

I was grateful for a chance to hide my face. I could feel it already burning bright red with embarrassment, and I was pretty sure Fletcher wouldn't have said it was cute.

"God, thank you for pulling us all together," Tobey prayed. "I don't know about anybody else, but I felt like a magnet was bringing me here today. It's like we're being faced with our biggest challenge yet, and we can't do it without You. Please be with us. Give us wisdom, strength, courage. And especially, please, God, be with Cheyenne. Make her know that she isn't alone, no matter what her trouble is. Help us to stand beside her without flinching, without even blinking. We ask this in Christ's name."

"Amen," we all murmured.

Then it was my turn. Nobody said, "Go, Cheyenne." They just looked at me. Shannon took hold of my hand. Brianna nodded to me from across the circle.

This was it. I looked down at the floor tiles, and I told my story.

When I was done, it was so quiet, so heavy quiet, I couldn't stand it. I took a breath and went on talking. "I know none of you would ever do anything as stupid as this," I said. "You don't have to act like I'm on the same level as you. I understand if you don't respect me anymore—"

"You can just knock off that kind of talk right now." Brianna's dark eyes were flashing. They swept the circle, setting everybody to nodding.

"Yeah," I said, "but none of you—"

"None of us what—ever did anything we were ashamed of?" Norie said. "You have to be kidding. I used to cheat, remember? And back in November, I'd have done it again, big-time, if the circumstances had been different. Come on, we've all messed up."

"You didn't know me before, girl," Brianna said. "I used to smoke marijuana every weekend when we lived in Oakland. I thought I was tough. I used to get into so many fights—till nobody would fight me anymore because they knew I'd kick their tail. You wouldn't have given me a second look."

"But that was back when you were a kid," I said.

"A whole three years ago. Mmm-hmm."

"We've all done stuff we're ashamed of," Tobey said. She sparkled out a grin. "Except maybe Shannon."

"I have!" Shannon said. "And it wasn't any three years ago either. I feel so dirty sometimes after I have a fight with my sister. I start out with all these thoughts like I'm really going to be patient and all that, and then I end up swearing at her and calling her stuff you wouldn't believe."

"Come on, Chey," Norie said. "You can't let that stop you from accepting our help."

"And more important," Ms. Race said, "God's help."

"God," I said. I breathed out so hard my bangs lifted and then fell flat to my forehead again. "I don't know, you guys. I've disappointed God so many times—"

"Who among us hasn't?" Ms. Race said. "Girls, I'm thirty-five years old. I consider myself a strong Christian. But don't think for a minute I haven't let God down. That doesn't make it all right, but honey, you have to know that just because you aren't perfect doesn't mean God isn't still there for you."

"Can I ask a question?" Marissa said.

They all looked at me, and I shrugged. "Sure," I said.

"Why did you steal? It just seems like if you knew why, you'd see that it isn't because you're a terrible person."

"Good thought," Ms. Race said.

Nobody tried to make me come up with an explanation. I even sat there for a minute hoping they would move onto another subject. Where was that topic fairy when you needed her?

Then finally I sighed. "I just wanted to fit in," I said. It sounded so pathetic I wanted to bite it back the minute I said it.

"What do you mean, 'fit in'?" Norie said. "You're one of us!"

"Not really," I said. "Think about it. I don't have money like you guys do. So I can't dress the way you do, or buy people presents—"

"Wait a minute," Brianna said. She looked across the circle at Marissa. "You have money, girl?"

Marissa gave her soft little laugh and shook her head. "My father is out of work every time it snows because he's a brick-layer. We eat so many beans in the winter!"

"And you've obviously never been to my place," Brianna said. "My mama and me live in a one-bedroom apartment at the other end of Seventh Street. You know that park on the corner? We have homeless people wandering over from there all the time, knocking on our door, and half the time we ask them if they have something to share! My mama uses food stamps, girl." She leaned way over toward me and stuck her eyes to my face. "And you know something, Cheyenne? There's no shame in being poor. The only shame is in thinking you're less than everybody else because you don't have a lot of money to throw around. It takes me two months to save ten extra dollars from my baby-sitting after I help my mama with the rent. But you don't see me hanging my head like I'm not every bit as good as every person in this group, do you?"

I shook my head. I didn't trust myself to talk.

"My parents aren't exactly rolling in it either," Shannon said. She played with a strand of her silky blond hair. "My mother makes all my clothes now because they're paying out so much for psychiatrists and stuff for my sister."

"And it doesn't bother you that much, right?" Norie said.

"What bothers me is when other people give me these weird looks because my jeans don't have the right label on them or something." Shannon's eyes got big. "You guys never make me feel that way. It's those other people."

"Jackals," Norie said.

"They're just a bunch of losers!" I said. "I always thought you and Brianna and Marissa were totally as rich as Norie or Tobey."

"That's because they act rich," Norie said. "Not like snobby but just like they believe in themselves."

Tobey directed her brown eyes at me, and her face went soft. "God thinks you're cool. Why can't we just go on from there?"

"Go where?" I said.

There was a pause. Ms. Race cleared her throat. "I don't usually say 'this is the thing to do,' but in this case, I can see only one path to take."

Her face was so sober, my chest started to tighten. This wasn't sounding good already.

"You're saying I should turn myself in, aren't you?" I said.

"What, like to the police?" Tobey said.

"She didn't commit a murder!" Norie said. "Could we use different words or something?"

"Confession," Marissa said softly.

"I like that," Ms. Race said. "I think it's more a matter of asking for forgiveness from the right person rather than throwing yourself on the mercy of the court."

"That lady in the shop was really nice, Cheyenne," Tobey said.

I sat up ramrod straight. "You mean Angel Lady?"

"Uh, what?" Norie said.

I waved her off. "You mean I have to go in and tell her what I did—and say I'm sorry?"

"Aren't you?" Brianna said.

"Yes! I wish I'd never done it; it was the stupidest thing on the planet. But that lady is like this angel. I don't know if I can face her. She kept calling me 'dear'!"

"Maybe she *is* an angel," Shannon said.

"Ooh, weird," Norie said.

"No, I mean, she's *like* an angel," Shannon said.

Ms. Race nodded thoughtfully. "And if she is, she'll forgive you, Cheyenne."

"But what if she doesn't? What if she calls the cops? I'll be back in Wittenberg so fast!"

"For a handful of beads?" Norie said. "No offense, Cheyenne. Brianna, don't listen to this. But we can't be talking about more than five or six dollars worth of stuff."

"What if we take up a collection from just us, and we offer to pay the lady for it?" Tobey said.

"I can't do that," I said. My chest was pressing down hard. "I don't have any way to pay you back."

"Sure you do," Ms. Race said. "You can work for me. You have this Saturday free?"

"Yeah," I said.

Brianna grunted. "Or do you have to do homework?"

I looked miserably at the floor.

"Hey, none of that," Brianna said. "You hold your head high, girl. You're about to do a brave thing; now give yourself credit for that."

"I wouldn't have to do it if I hadn't stolen in the first place."

"Uh-huh," Brianna said, her voice dry. "And I wouldn't be missing so many of my brain cells if I hadn't smoked so much dope. But I don't have time to waste thinking about that, and neither do you."

I put my head in my hands and rested my elbows on my knees. "I'm so confused," I said.

"Let me try to clear things up for you," Ms. Race said. Her voice was smooth and calm, and just hearing it, I have to admit, got me breathing again.

"First, we all lay our hands on you while you ask God to forgive you. And then you don't expect this immediate religious experience." She grinned at me. "Then we supply the money and a couple of the girls go with you to the shop while the rest of us pray. The lady is not going to throw you in jail, Cheyenne. I can guarantee you that, but if it will make you feel any better, I'll be there, outside, just in case there's trouble. You have no idea how much better you're going to feel after you do this. And then we are going to help you so you are never tempted to do anything like this again. Fair enough?"

It did sound fair. And like it could actually happen. I felt my lips coming apart in an almost-smile. But just as fast, I felt them sag.

"What's wrong now?" Norie said.

"What about Tassie?" I said. "Should I tell her before I go to the shop?"

"Do you think you should?" Ms. Race said.

"It feels like I'm being dishonest if I don't."

"Then what's the problem?" Tobey said.

Tears splashed down onto my hands, and they felt hot and angry on my skin. "I don't know what she has to do if I tell her I've committed a crime. She always follows the foster-care rules. She might have to turn me in."

They weren't so sure about that one. Nope, none of them had had the run-ins with the law that I'd had. It was like I was speaking a foreign language or something. We all found ourselves looking at Ms. Race.

"I'm very comfortable with keeping this just among us for now," Ms. Race said. "One step at a time, huh!"

There was a bunch of relieved nodding. I couldn't nod with them.

"What is up with you, Cheyenne?" Norie said. "What are you, the eternal pessimist?"

"I'm just scared, that's all," I said. "I can't help it. Except for meeting you guys and living at Tassie's, nothing in my life has ever turned out right. It's hard to believe in it."

"Interesting, isn't it?" Ms. Race said.

"Okay," Norie said, "what?"

"That the only good things in your life have happened now that you're turning to God. I don't think that's a coincidence."

"I don't even believe in coincidence," Brianna said. "It's all God, far as I can see."

"You are so cool, Brianna," Tobey said.

"Then will you go with me to the shop?" I blurted out.

Brianna looked at me like I was completely nuts. "Of course I'm going to go with you, girl. Who else do you think cares more about you than I do?"

"Me," Tobey said. She gave me a big, soft smile. "I want to go, too."

"Are we taking up a collection?" Shannon said.

"Forget it," Norie said. "I have it handled."

"This is glorious," Ms. Race said.

Everybody bobbed their heads and started putting their hands on me, and we prayed. All I could say was thank you, though I wasn't quite sure why—God hadn't performed the miracle yet. But I said it anyway. And the weird thing was, I felt better.

CHAPTER NINE

THE POLE GIRLS WERE PRETTY SMART. THEY WANTED to take me to the shop the next day. They didn't say it, but I knew they didn't want to give me a chance to freak out and run the other way. Go figure.

But I didn't even think about running. Now there was a plan and maybe a spark of hope—about the size of a pea, but it was there. The only thing that got my chest to pressing in on itself was that the next day at school Fletcher seemed to be everywhere.

I'm not kidding, I couldn't turn around without practically falling over him. I got to my locker that morning and there he was, hanging out by the trash can like it was the trendy place to be.

"Hi, Chey," he said. He made a face and started to talk in this high-pitched voice. "Hi, Chey. How dorky does that sound?' He made his voice go deep. "Hello, Cheyenne. How art thou?"

I wanted to giggle. I wanted to run over there and make dumb rhymes with him. But I didn't trust myself not to blurt out, "I'm a thief. You don't want me!"

So I waved and went on down the hall. I couldn't resist a glance back though, and there he was, still watching me. He waved and backed up, right into the trash can. Both of them crashed to the ground. A bunch of people started to clap. But I was a truly loyal friend and disappeared into the mob.

In Spanish fourth period, it was like he hadn't embarrassed himself in front of the entire freshman locker hall. I was figuring out that Fletcher just didn't get embarrassed. He was that cool. In class he kept passing my desk to go to the pencil sharpener, and every time he would either pretend to bump my arm accidentally, pull my hair, or try to stick the pencil in my ear. He made so many trips *Señora* Diaz told him to start using a pen. It was about the first time I ever wanted to thank the woman for anything. I could hardly stand having to ignore him so I wouldn't blow it.

So what does he do? At lunch in the theater lobby, after the Girls prayed me up for that afternoon, he shows up and plops himself right down beside me.

"So," he said, "where's my bracelet?"

I turned into an Eskimo pie. I mean it, my heart stopped beating, and I quit breathing. It was this horrible, frozen moment.

"Could you be any more rude, Fletcher?" Tobey said. "You don't go around asking people for presents!"

I could have kissed her boots—if my lips hadn't been frozen.

"She doesn't care," Fletcher said. "She's my amino!" He did that little head-shaking thing that made his silky hair go all over the place and started a smile. Then he slung his arm around my shoulders and left it draped there. At that point, I think my brain stopped functioning.

"I'm not even going to ask," Norie said. "Last time I heard, an amino was some kind of body acid, but that's okay. Call her whatever you want to."

Fortunately Wyatt appeared just then, and Norie pretty much forgot anybody else was there. I wanted to do that with Fletcher, too. I'd daydreamed about something like this happening almost since the first time I caught that long, slow smile, and now here he was with his arm around me, giving me a nickname and thinking I was cute—and I couldn't do a thing about it.

Sure, I wanted to hang with him. I wanted to pass notes in the halls, talk for hours on the phone, listen to all the off-the-wall stuff he was always saying. But there was no way. If he ever found out what had happened, forget it. The Girls' understanding, that was one thing. But not Fletcher. It was just different.

Okay, that wasn't entirely true. I was scared spitless—I mean, like right out of my Kmart overalls. What if we got together, and we had this neat thing going. Then what if he discovered I was a former shoplifter? What then?

I'll tell you what then. Pain. And I'd already had enough pain from the people I loved to last me my whole life. I wasn't going to walk right into it.

Still holding my breath, I inched away from Fletcher. I didn't look at him; I concentrated on something else across the circle. It took me a second to realize it was Brianna—and that she was cocking one of her thin, classy eyebrows at me.

Don't ask, Brianna, I thought. *'Cause I'll start bawlin' for sure.*

Fletcher seemed to take the hint right away, and he got up and left. I didn't watch him go. My heart was already breaking.

Anyway, the Plan of Action went like this: Shannon, Marissa, and Norie went to Marissa's house to pray and wait for the rest of us to come back. I was praying, too: that we would end up there and not at the police station. Oh, ye of little faith, huh?

Ms. Race drove Tobey, Brianna, and me to the strip mall. I sat in back with Tobey reassuring me. Still, Brianna had to practically drag me out when we arrived.

"I feel good about this, Cheyenne," Ms. Race said before Tobey closed the car door. "With all this prayer going on, how can you lose?"

I honestly couldn't answer her. I'd never had this much prayer going on before.

If Tobey and Brianna thought I was going to bolt, they

didn't show it. They gave me plenty of space as we walked up to the door of the bead shop. My legs were shaking so bad I was wobbling, but my insides were even more unstable. Just as Brianna put her hand on the door handle, I said, "Stop."

I could feel them looking at each other over my head.

"What's wrong?" Tobey said.

"I don't know," I said. "I've just never been this scared in my life. I feel like I'm about to lose it."

"I felt that way a lot last fall," Tobey said. "I found out it's when you feel the weakest that God's the strongest. It's weird, but it works that way."

"I don't get it," I said.

Brianna squeezed my arm. "You don't have to. Just have a little faith for once, okay? It's going to be all right."

"Do you really believe that?" I said. I was barely talking above a whisper.

"No," she said.

I *was* ready to bolt then.

"I don't just believe it," she said. "I know it. Now are you ready?"

My legs kept shaking. But when she opened the door, I managed to get inside the shop and up to the counter.

I saw right away that Angel Lady was in the store, straightening up some chains on their pegs. She was humming under her breath and nodding her braided head in time, like she was in some kind of magical world of her own.

Once I saw her I knew there was no turning back. At least there wasn't anybody else in the shop to hear my pitiful confession. Except for the Shop Sitter, who was behind the counter reading a newspaper as if he hadn't moved since the last time I'd been there. He didn't even seem to see us. But Angel Lady did.

"Well, my dear!" she said. Her face lit up like she had just switched on her halo. Her eyes, though, were all concerned. I almost expected her to come over and feel my forehead.

"Are you all right?" she said. "The way you ran out of here on Friday, I thought something was terribly wrong!"

"No, I'm all right," I said.

"Good. I'm glad to hear it."

She stood there with her hands clasped in front of her gently rounded tummy and kept smiling. I wondered what her face was going to look like when it was mad. For an awful second I saw my mother's face on her body, baggy-eyed and looking at me out of drunken, hate-filled eyes.

I felt a soft nudge in my side. I looked up at Brianna, who was giving me a firm stare. Okay. It was time.

I took in a deep breath, but I forgot to let it out. I wiped my sweaty hands up and down on the sides of my overalls and tried to get my head to stop spinning.

Then suddenly I felt somebody take hold of my right hand, and somebody else got my left. Brianna and Tobey were hanging onto me. But not to keep me from making a run for it. This sounds cheesy, but I just felt like it was so I could feel their prayers coming into me. It got my mouth to open.

"Um, I'm all right," I said again.

Angel Lady nodded.

"But there was something wrong on Friday when I was in here."

"Oh." She knitted her eyebrows together. "What, dear? I don't understand."

I took in more air, without ever letting the first breath out. "Those beads I picked out, the ones that fell all over the floor?"

"Yes?"

"I was—before you came in—I was going to take them. You know, without paying for them."

I was aware that the newspaper was rustling behind the counter, but I couldn't take my eyes off Angel Lady. She didn't get it yet, I was sure, because she was still looking at me with all this worry in her eyes. Any minute now I knew it was going to dawn on her, and she was going to explode. I wanted to get it out before that happened.

"You remember when I was in here before?" I said. "With two girls? I took some beads then. See, she's wearing them. I wanted her to have a present, and I didn't have any money, and I didn't plan to come in here and rip you off, but it just happened, and I feel like a jerk about it, and I just wanted to come in here and apologize and pay you for them and ask you to forgive me and please not to call the police or anything because I am never going to do anything like that again. We've been praying so hard, and I think God forgives me and I just . . . please . . . will you . . . too?"

I hadn't planned on crying, and I wasn't sobbing or anything. A tear just splashed out of control down onto my overalls.

Angel Lady's expression still didn't change. I figured she was too shocked to move. Shop Sitter, on the other hand, slapped down his newspaper on the counter and cleared his throat like he was trying to cough up a hairball. Angel Lady gave him a look kind of like the ones Tassie gave us when we were being rude at the table. He shut up.

Angel Lady looked back at me. I was about to turn blue from not breathing, but I figured it wasn't worth it if she pressed charges. I'd just as soon drop dead right there on the floor.

"You're very brave," Angel Lady said finally.

I could feel Tobey squeezing my hand.

"And let me say this," she went on, "I do forgive you. That's what a Christian does, now, isn't it?"

I didn't even think about it. I just nodded. Hope was bubbling up in me like a water fountain.

"You know something, my dear, I was quite taken with you right from the start," she said. "I watched you while you were looking around that first day. You really love the beautiful things, don't you?"

I nodded.

"You aren't a bad girl, anybody can see that. Otherwise, you wouldn't even have come back here today."

"That's right," Tobey said.

But before she could go on, Angel Lady held up a blue-veined hand. "I just want to hear it from the horse's mouth," she said. "Now, my dear, what's your name?"

"Cheyenne," I said, though I'm sure she would have to turn up her hearing aid to catch it.

She closed her eyes and smiled a little lined smile. "That's lovely; that's perfect for you. Now, Cheyenne," She opened her eyes. "I want you to tell me one thing."

"Okay," I said. I'd have told her the formula for the atom bomb if I'd known it.

"I want you to tell me why you stole from me," she said.

For what seemed like the thousandth time, I spilled it: how much I wanted to belong and be like the other Girls; how lousy I'd have felt if I hadn't had a gift for Brianna. I even had Brianna take off the earrings so Angel Lady could have a close look.

The whole time, she listened like I was the president or something, and she just kept nodding and working the lines in her face and clasping and unclasping the map-veined hands. My hopes were rising, big-time. When I was done, she smiled and sent them even higher.

"Oh, I hear what you're saying," she said. "I know what it is to want to give of yourself so much, you'll do just about anything."

"You do?" I said. I smacked away the tears from my face.

"I do. I think most of us do." She held up a softly gnarled finger. "But you're only stealing your own chances for a good life. Whatever is meant to be will be if you let it."

"I will!" I said. My voice sounded like it had just been let out of a cage. I knew I was kind of out of control, but I couldn't help it. This sounded like "everything is okay" to me. I wanted to wrap my arms around it, you know?

"I am never going to steal anything ever again!" I said.

"Especially not my own life. I like how you said that; that's so cool. Thank you so much for not being mad at me. I don't think I could have stood it. I mean, not just because I didn't want to go back to Wittenberg, but you were so nice to me, it's really awful to hurt somebody that's nice, you know? But you—"

"Wait a minute. Wait just a minute."

We all turned our heads toward the counter. Shop Sitter was standing up, leaning on the glass—right there where the sign said, *Please Do Not Lean on Glass*—and he was glaring at us. With Julius eyes. I took a step back and tromped on Tobey's toe.

The man opened his mouth again, though it looked more like a gash in his face than a mouth.

"Did you say *back* to Wittenberg?" he said.

"That's what she said, Sam," Angel Lady said. "Why? What difference does it make?"

"Wittenberg's a prison!" he said.

"It's not a prison!"

That came from Brianna. She put her hands on her hips. "I don't mean to be rude, but you need to get your facts straight," she said.

"Well, if not a prison, what?" Angel Lady said.

For the first time, she was looking uncertain. I felt like somebody was hitting my chest with a two by four.

"It's like a juvenile shelter," Brianna said.

"It's like a juvenile jail, is what it is!" Sam said out of his rip of a mouth. "They put all the incorrigibles out there!"

"I'm not an incorrigible!" I cried. "I don't even know what that is!"

"It's kids who are so bad there's no more hope for them!" Sam said. His eyes were old-man watery and red, and he turned them on Angel Lady. "She's the worst kind, Elena. Tryin' to make you think she's full of remorse, but all the time she's laughing up her sleeve." He nodded toward Tobey. "She had you fooled, too, did she? You oughta be careful about hanging around with kids like her."

"No sir," Tobey said. Her voice was strong and clear, but Sam waved her off like she had just tried to tell him I was Joan of Arc. Once again he turned to his wife while my chest caved in.

"Don't be a nincompoop, Elena," he said. "I'm calling the police." His watery eyes fixed on me. "That's the only way we're ever going to get rid of people like her."

CHAPTER
TEN

I NEVER BELIEVED IT WHEN PEOPLE CLAIMED THEY
saw their lives flash before their eyes when they were drown-
ing or something. But as I stood there watching Sam the Shop
Sitter reach for the telephone, I actually had a vision of my
whole life sliding away from me.

Living at Tassie's.

Having a brother like Diesel and a sister like Felise.

Being friends with the Flagpole Girls.

Having a chance to finally make it in school.

Feeling like a halfway worthwhile person.

It hit me like a pair of headlights on high beam: I had this
incredible life, and now it was about to be snatched away
from me with one phone call.

I was screaming, "No! Please!" before I even realized it.

It didn't even faze Sam. He just kept punching buttons.

"I know I deserve to be punished," I pleaded with him.
"I'll take any punishment you guys give me, but please don't
bring in the police. Just—*please!*"

"Sam," said a sharp voice.

Sam stopped and looked at Elena.

"Put down the phone," she said. "There's no need for
that."

He stopped punching and looked at her for a whole
minute. I drew blood on my bottom lip.

Finally he hung up.

"You let people walk all over you," he said to Elena. Angrily, he snatched up the *Gazette-Journal* and made a stiff beeline for the back room.

Elena winced a little when the door slammed behind him, but her eyes were kind as she looked at me. "There will be no police, Cheyenne," she said. "I'll take your money, and I'll let you go, if you promise that you will never, ever throw your chances away like this again."

"I promise," I said.

Tobey opened her purse and took out the twenty-dollar bill Norie had given her.

"I'm sure that's far too much," Elena said.

"We want you to have it," Tobey said. Norie had told us not to come back with any change or we were dog chow. You didn't argue with Norie.

"The change goes into my emergency fund then," Elena said. She folded it neatly and put it in her pocket. "I try to keep a little money tucked away in case anybody's really in need. Most of my friends are on fixed incomes. The price of one prescription can wipe them out for a month."

I'm not sure I heard any of that. My heart was doing this loud, relief-beat thing in my chest, which hadn't caved in after all. I did hear Elena's parting words to us though.

"There's an old Irish proverb," she said when we had jangled open the door. " 'Better one good thing that is, than two good things that were or three good things that might never come to pass.' " She crinkled her eyes at me. "You remember that, Cheyenne. And pray. If you do, you'll never steal again."

I could hardly stand to leave. As it was, I threw my arms around her neck. She held me there, and I was pretty sure her eyes were wet when we left.

I have to tell you, I never felt so free my whole life. Not the day they sprung me from Wittenberg. Not the day they arrested Julius and my mother. Not even the day I ran away from my second foster home. When they say your heart can sing . . . well, it's true.

Ms. Race knew before we even jumped into the car. Must have been the ear-to-ear grin I was wearing, or possibly the little end-zone dance I performed on the sidewalk.

"Thank you, *God!*" she said when we climbed in.

"It was awesome," Tobey said. "That lady was like this total Christian."

"Her husband sure wasn't," Brianna said. Her dark eyes were still stormy. "I thought I was going to have to show him what time it was."

We talked all over each other telling Ms. Race about it, so by the time we pulled in at Marissa's, we were completely hyper. Marissa, Norie, and Shannon blasted out of the house, jumped up and down with us, and squealed—until Norie took a dive on the ice. Ms. Race said she thought we all ought to get inside before we had to have the celebration in the emergency room at Washoe Med.

It wasn't until we reached the front porch that it registered in me that our together, well-dressed Marissa lived in an even smaller house than mine. It was in an older section of town near UNR. In fact, most of the houses around there were rented out to broke college students who all had at least one window boarded up and at least one piece of thrown-away furniture lying around outside with its stuffings belching out.

But inside, it smelled like melted cheese and spices, and just being in there made my mouth water. I guess I hadn't really gotten a whole meal down in days.

"What is that divine aroma?" Ms. Race said.

She went into the micro-kitchen where an older copy of Marissa and a bunch of brown kids were milling. I looked around the living room while Marissa collected coats.

There wasn't that much furniture—just the usual couch, chair, and coffee table. But it seemed full, comfortable full, like you wanted to throw yourself down and kick back. There were mounds of pillows in bright colors. Once I took a closer look, I saw they were hand-painted, sort of Southwestern style. They reminded me of the kind of thing my mother used to make at the artists' co-op in Winnemucca, before she married Julius. I hadn't thought about that in a long time. And I didn't want to now.

I shook myself back to the homeyness of Marissa's house, and for the first time realized a cool Latin beat was coming out of a tape deck on the floor—and that not a thing there had come from Macy's. It was wonderful, like being at Tassie's, where *I* lived.

Marissa's mother came in then with these big casseroles of chili rellenos and enchiladas, and we gathered around the coffee table and ate until our eyes were streaming from the chili powder and the jalapeños. It was great.

While we pigged out, my story got told, and when the last detail was spun, Norie nodded in that middle-aged-wise-lady way she had. "That was better than any sermon I ever heard," she said. "It's like, yikes, decent people are actually out there in the world."

"I'm so happy for you, Cheyenne," Shannon said. "I'd give about anything if my sister would make amends with everybody she's hurt and start over like you are."

"Is that what I did?" I said.

"It is," Ms. Race said. "I hadn't put it together that way, but you're right."

"Oh yeah," Norie said. "My dad—you know, the recovering alcoholic—did that. It's, like, step nine or something."

"Wow," Tobey said. "You're advanced, Cheyenne."

"I think we better pray," Brianna said. "This is way too big for my little mind."

So we held salsa-stained hands and prayed, and I know I prayed like I never had before. It just burst out of me, kind of like a song in the shower. "God," I said, "I don't even have the words to thank You—and You know if *I* don't have the words, it's huge! You saved my life. I promise You, I will never let You down again."

When we all raised our heads again, I felt like a different person than I had that morning as I'd crawled out of bed all churned up with fear. What I was feeling was unfamiliar. Now I know I was simply grateful. Then all I knew was that it felt good.

We hung around at Marissa's for a while, eating sopapillas, which are these pockets of fried sweet bread filled with jam that are to die for. Everybody was listening to some story Norie was telling about something she read when Tobey scooted close to me and whispered, "Can I talk to you about Fletcher?"

For the first time since we left the bead store, I felt a twinge in my chest again.

"What about him?" I said.

"He came in my room last night—and I mean, he never comes in my room unless I have food in there. He wanted to know if you were mad at him."

"No," I said. "Why would I be mad?"

"Beats me, but get this: He goes, 'I can be a jerk sometimes. Did she say I said something jerky to her?'"

I already knew what he was talking about. I was the one who had been the jerk.

"He didn't exactly ask me to find out," Tobey was saying. "But I thought I'd ask you. I mean, he is my brother. If he was being a dork to you, it would be good to know so I could pound him."

"No, he's rad!" I said. "He can do anything and not seem like a geek. When he smiles that way, like he does, you know, real slow, I about go nuts. You're his sister so you don't see it, but he's totally a hunk, Tobe."

Tobey didn't smile, but I could tell she was having a hard time keeping her face straight, just from the way her eyes started to do that dance thing. "Well," she said, "if that's the way you feel, he doesn't think you act like it. He said when he, like, put his arm around you yesterday, you acted as if he had leprosy."

"He doesn't!" I said stupidly.

"Well, cooties, maybe—and definitely some bad B.O. once in a while." She shrugged. "I guess it was just his imagination. He tends to wig out."

"Hey, L'Orange," Norie said. "What's that chick's name who's the editor of *Brio* magazine?"

They drifted off into some conversation about stuff I'd never heard of, and at that moment could have cared less about. What was important was that it bugged Fletcher I had blown him off.

Then I stopped myself. What good did that do me? Just because Elena had forgiven me and the whole shoplifting ordeal was over didn't mean I hadn't stolen in the first place. What was I going to say to Fletcher if I was his girlfriend and he one day said, "Hey, I heard you stole something."

"Sure, Fletch, but it's okay. They let me off."

Yeah right.

This way, I'd never have to see that look in his eye people get when they find out stuff about you when they had thought you were this angel. What was that saying? "Better to have loved and lost than never to have loved at all." No way. Whoever wrote that didn't know what he was talking about.

I rode home with Ms. Race, and she dropped me off last. I gave her this big ol' hug in the driveway, and she laughed into my hair.

"You are something, Cheyenne," she said. "I'm so proud of you."

I pulled back and looked at her solemnly. "Don't forget, I have to work off the money."

"I haven't forgotten. Saturday."

"Right."

"Nine A.M. and wear your grubbies."

I'd have worn football pads and a tutu if she had asked me to. This grateful stuff was making a new person out of me.

The rest of the week I was walking around on air currents, although I admit I wasn't exactly floating when I was avoiding Fletcher. But I figured if I just wasn't around him, he would move onto some lucky girl who didn't have a past.

It was hard to do in Spanish where he sat two rows over. I impressed *Señora* Diaz right out of her *zapatas* by keeping my face buried in my book or my head bent over my assignment. She even told me she was giving me some extra points for effort.

It didn't work on Fletcher the first day. He shot a spitball at me when she stepped out of the room, passed me a note that said, *¿Hey, qué pasa, amino?* and dove across three other people to get to me when *Señora* Diaz said to find a dialogue partner. There wasn't much I could do about that. But after sitting across from him for fifteen minutes and not saying anything unless it was in *español*, I think I convinced him I didn't want to talk to him because the rest of the week he didn't even look at me. By Friday I was having to scold myself to keep from thinking, *Maybe this is worse than if we had gotten together and then . . .*

Nope. Couldn't take the chance. Too much pain.

I didn't do pain.

Saturday I had Ms. Race to think about, and that helped. Since she had told me to wear grubbies, I was pretty sure I'd be washing her windows or her car or something. I didn't have to dig far in my wardrobe to find something that looked ratty. Most of my *good* stuff Norie or Tobey would have cleaned the furnace in—or with.

When I walked into the living room at 8:55, after whipping through my own chores, I was in ripped jeans, a T-shirt with a spaghetti sauce stain on it, and a flannel you could practically see through in spots. Tassie looked up from the kitchen table where she was writing out checks and raised both eyebrows. Not a good sign.

"You're going out with your teacher in *that?*" she said.

"Sure," I said.

But I felt an uneasy flutter in my chest. I still hadn't told Tassie about the shoplifting thing. How was I going to explain that I was doing a payback for Ms. Race without telling her what I was paying her back *for*? Ugh. Keeping secrets now wasn't as easy as it used to be. *Maybe I should just go ahead and tell her,* I thought.

But she cut that good thought off with her next choice of topic. "Have you written your mother yet?"

I drew my hands up into the sleeves of my flannel and crossed my arms over my chest. "No," I said. "Do I have to?"

"It would be the thing to do," Tassie said.

"The thing to do" was stuff like homework, chores, and not staying out past curfew. I wasn't going to have any choice.

The thought stuck in my chest like a piece of meat that wouldn't go down. But at least it helped me decide one thing: I wasn't going to tell Tassie about what had happened. There was still the chance she would have to inform the foster-care people. And Tassie's mentioning my mother, now in the halfway house, gave me another chilling thought. They might not send me back to Wittenberg. They might make me live with my mother.

No way. No way, no how.

CHAPTER ELEVEN

MS. RACE'S TIMING WAS PERFECT. SHE PULLED INTO the driveway just then, and I was out of there like my ragbag jeans were on fire.

God, I prayed silently as I careened across the ice to her car, *could we go back to my being grateful now? I liked that better.*

As always, He was true to His promises. Sometimes I hate it when that happens.

Ms. Race's little Honda looked pretty clean already. That was cool. I'd do windows at her house; I couldn't wait to see where she lived.

After I climbed in and we got the hi-how-are-ya's out of the way, I said, "Norie says you have a neat place."

She looked a little surprised. "That's nice of her. What brought that on?"

"Aren't we going there?" I said.

She shook her head, and I noticed that the usual French braid didn't move because she had her hair all tucked up under a ball cap. She looked kind of young and cute—for thirty-five, anyway.

"Oh," I said. "Where are we going?"

"To the Mental Health Center over off Glendale," she said.

I felt sick like I always did whenever government institutions were involved.

"What are we going there for?" I said. "You know, Felise—

that's one of my foster sisters—well, the only one I would actually claim as a sister—she had to go there to a shrink for a while. She says he made her feel crazier than she did before she started. Tassie told him after Felise came to stay with her that Felise didn't need him anymore. And that was true—I think it's true for me, too. Not that I couldn't have used a psychiatrist at times—I do get a little nuts—but I'm way over that now."

"Cheyenne," Ms Race said, "would you chill, darlin'? I'm not taking you there to see a shrink."

"Oh," I said. "Whew."

She laughed her low chuckle that seemed like it came from way down in her throat. "But don't go off like that too much while we're there or somebody will think you're a patient."

"Why are we going there?" I said.

"To do some work for the Salvation Army."

I drew a blank. "Isn't it a little late to dress up like Santa Claus?" All I knew about the Salvation Army was those guys who rang bells in the malls from Thanksgiving to Christmas Eve.

Ms. Race was about to bust an intestine laughing. "Cheyenne, you are too funny. We aren't going to play Santa. We're going to feed some hungry people."

I have to admit, I wasn't all that excited. I mean, come on, I'd been all psyched up to spend a day alone with this really cool lady that I usually had to compete with five other girls to get a word from, and now she was telling me we were headed for some kind of soup kitchen. It was hard to be excited about something that depressing.

But I thought it would be rude to show it, so I just said, "Oh. Cool." I sneaked a glance at the car clock. 9:15. Lunch would be over at, what, one o'clock? Could I keep on a fake smile for three and a half hours? I caught myself and prayed quickly, *God, uh, could You help me out here?*

The building where lunch was served was empty except

for four people lying around in the lounge. One was staring at a dog-eared paperback novel, and the rest were staring at the TV, which was blaring out cartoons. I had the chilly feeling that none of them were really absorbed with what they were looking at.

"Why are they here?" I whispered to Ms. Race as we carried our boxes into the kitchen.

"They have some problems," she told me. "The people who work here try to get them to the point where they can function on their own."

I peered through the window in the door at the lounge. "I don't think that's going to happen," I said.

"You would be surprised. A couple of them look better than they did last month, if you can believe that."

The whole place suddenly made me think of my mother, trying to get her life together in a halfway house so she could "function on her own."

I turned from the window with a jerk and said, "Okay, what do you want me to do?"

We spent about an hour cleaning up the kitchen, which was pretty cruddy. While we scrubbed and scoured, we talked about a bunch of stuff. I mostly asked a lot of questions, and Ms. Race told me about her girls' Sunday school class back in Chicago and how she went on a mission trip to a Third-World country every summer and how blessed she felt to have the Flagpole Girls to love.

"We totally love you, too," I said.

She smiled, but she didn't answer. We started to peel potatoes, and she commented on what an incredible cook Marissa was.

"I think she gets it from her mother," Ms. Race said.

Could we please talk about something besides mothers? I wanted to say.

By noon, we had the whole meal set up, just the two of us, and if I do say so myself, it looked like a feast. We had this big stack of plates, a pyramid of plastic forks wrapped in napkins, and a basket overflowing with buns. Our pots were all lined up ready to ladle from when people came up to the serving window. I was practically drooling into the pots, they smelled so good: mashed potatoes, slices of roast beef, gravy, and peas.

"They can come back up for brownies after we've served everyone the hot stuff," Ms. Race said.

I eyed the brownies in question. *If I don't eat most of them myself before that,* I thought.

About five after twelve, somebody unlocked the front doors, and suddenly I couldn't hear the TV for the voices. I figured out right off that hungry people shout a lot.

"Man your ladles, Cheyenne," Ms. Race said. "Here they come."

I expected this mass shove to the window like kids trying to get in at a rock concert—so I'd heard. I'd never actually been to one.

But even though everybody seemed to be yelling to each other, they formed two pretty orderly lines in front of the window. Most of the guys took off their ball caps, which were so grimy you couldn't read what was printed on them. Their hair wasn't much better underneath. I don't like to own up to it, but I immediately started to think about lice.

But, dude, were they polite. The first guy took his plate, all heaped with food, and stared at it like the steam was putting him in a trance.

"Is everything all right?" I said. "Oh, you didn't get a roll."

I put a warm biscuit on his plate, and he looked at me out of these eyes that seemed really far away. "Thank you," he said. "Thank you so much."

They were all that way. They might have been scary-looking people, some of them, with eye patches, or scars, or voices like gravel, but most were more polite than any kid I'd ever seen get a plate in the school cafeteria. Tassie would have been impressed, her being so hepped up about manners and everything.

It made me want to be nice to them.

"Is that enough peas?" I'd say. Or, "Do you want your gravy on your meat or on your potatoes? I like mine on my spuds, myself. You know, make a little hollow in there?"

The kids were my favorite. They wouldn't answer my questions with words, but they would nod or point, and they all smiled. This one little girl kept staring at my neck the whole time I was serving her. I put my hand up there to be sure I didn't have a booger hanging or something and realized she was looking at my bead necklace.

"You like this?" I said.

She nodded real shyly and hurried away with her plate.

Another lady had six kids with her. None of them could have been over seven. They started to chow down before they even left the window. It made me want to cry.

We must have filled about sixty plates before the room quieted. I looked out to see if they had all died of food poisoning or something, but they were just eating. It was evidently serious business.

"Where did they all come from?" I whispered to Ms. Race.

"The streets mostly," she said. "Which is why they talk so loud. They're used to shouting over the traffic. Some are from the homeless shelter. These are just the ones who heard about the food. A lot more just like them are out there somewhere." She peeked into the potato pot. "We still have some food left."

I leaned out the window and yelled, "There's more in here if anybody wants seconds!"

Several men shuffled up cautiously, and I tried to act like I was a cook in a diner as I loaded them up again, so they wouldn't feel ashamed. "You've got an appetite!" I said. "Enjoy!"

"You have a nice touch, Cheyenne," Ms. Race whispered to me. "You treat them with respect. They appreciate that."

"What about the brownies?" I said.

"I guess it's time."

She slid one of the trays onto the window counter, but I had an idea.

"Can I just walk around with these and serve them so they don't have to get up again?" I said. "They might feel more like they're in a restaurant that way. I mean, is that okay?"

"That's more than okay," Ms. Race said. "It's a great idea."

That was the best part of the whole thing. I carried a tray of brownies with one hand above my head and went from table to table. Then I'd lower the tray and let them pick out the one they wanted. The six kids looked like they had walked into Toys "R" Us with a gift certificate.

Speaking of which, when I was done serving the dessert, I noticed them getting down from the table and just wandering around.

"Don't they have any toys or anything?" I said to Ms. Race.

"Only what they might pull out of somebody's trash," she said. "Honey, they don't know where tonight's dinner is coming from. I think toys are the least of their worries."

"But kids need toys," I said. "Shoot, *I* need toys! A kid gets bored!"

"I know. It's a shame."

She picked up a pot and carried it to the sink. I stood there for a minute, fingering my earrings and thinking. It bugged me almost as much as the hunger. Even I had had some stuff to play with. My mother used to make dolls for me in Winnemucca—before Julius. I'd lugged one of them all the way to my second foster home—and then I'd gotten mad one day and had torn it up.

Dude, why do I keep coming back to my mother? I thought. I found myself tugging too hard on my earring, and I was about to shove my hands in my pockets when I thought of something.

I loved to fiddle with my jewelry when I was bored . . . I took off my earrings and my necklace and went back out into the lounge. The little girl who had been staring at my necklace was still sitting at the table next to her mother, kind of gazing blankly into space.

"Hi," I said to her. "What's your name?"

Her eyes lit up like little sparklers. "Tammi," she said.

"Would you like to have this?" I held out my hand with the necklace in it. She looked at it like I'd just said something to her in *español*.

She glanced at her mother, who was smoking a cigarette and staring uncertainly at my palm.

"It's okay, really," I said. "I want her to have it."

The mother shrugged and muttered a thank-you.

"Shall I put it on you?" I said.

Tammi nodded, about fifty times, and I put the necklace around her neck and fastened it. She tried to look down at it, but of course she couldn't see it. I took her by the hand, led her over to a window, and lifted her up so she could see her reflection. I think she would have stared all afternoon if my arms hadn't gotten tired.

When she went back to the table to show her mother again, I went off to find the six kids. They were taking turns holding each other up to drink out of the water fountain.

"Can you guys share?" I said.

They all scrambled around me and nodded. Every one of them had a runny nose like Niagara Falls. Dude, I wished I could have afforded children's Tylenol for all of them.

I held out what I did have though. They gaped down at the earrings and then at me and then at each other.

"It isn't that big a thing," I said. "I mean, I wish I had some, like, Tickle-Me Elmos or some Beanie Babies or something, but you can play with these. See, you want me to take them apart?"

But they all shook their heads. And when I said, "Go ahead, you can have them," the two oldest ones lifted them like they were something out of the lost Ark and walked off in awe. It was totally cool.

Everybody was gone by the time we cleaned up the kitchen. I kind of hated to see them go, although nobody left without coming to the window to say thank you one more time.

"You need help cleanin' up?" they would ask.

But we waved them on, told them to have a nice day. I was sure most of them had forgotten what a nice day was like.

"You earned your twenty dollars," Ms. Race said when we were walking to the car with our now much lighter boxes.

"I did?" I said.

"Uh, yeah—and then some. You worked hard in there."

"That's weird," I said. I looked back and watched the Mental Health Center disappear behind us as we pulled off down Glendale. "It didn't seem that much like work."

"I love the sound of that," Ms. Race said. "Did you get anything to eat?"

"No!" I said. "I wouldn't take their food!"

"Then I think I'd better feed you before I take you home. Do you like homemade soup?"

"Love it," I said. "Where do they serve that?"

"My house," she said. "But you can't come to the table dressed like that."

I looked down at my T-shirt and flannel, which were now spattered with gravy and smeared with chocolate. "I didn't bring any other clothes," I said.

"That's okay. I have something for you."

I had this neat tingle that I couldn't remember having before. I think it was anticipation. Until then, there hadn't been much in my life to look forward to.

I wasn't disappointed. When we reached Ms. Race's apartment, which was everything Norie had said it was, she told me to go in the bathroom and wash my hands and stuff—oh, and to put this on.

"This" was a purple T-shirt. I love purple. On the front it said, "Holy Hungers."

It fit me like it was made for me.

CHAPTER
TWELVE

"LOOKS GREAT ON YOU," MR. RACE SAID WHEN I came out. She was ladling soup into bowls on a checkered tablecloth on the floor. I sank down beside her onto a big pillow that looked like it had been made in Africa or something and stretched out the front of the shirt so I could look at it.

"I like it," I said. "I just don't know what it means."

Ms. Race crinkled her eyes at me. "Good," she said. "That gives us something to talk about."

I laughed into the glass of apple cider she handed me. "I don't usually have too much trouble with that!"

"If you want to know about the shirt, I'm going to have to start way back. Is that all right?"

"Sure. I might talk a lot, but I can also listen—I mean, you know, if it's interesting, which I know you'll be—you always are . . ." I stopped and rolled my eyes. "Just start talking, or I'll never shut up."

Ms. Race grinned while she chewed. Dude, she could still look like a lady even with her mouth full.

"Okay," she said finally. "When I first graduated from college, let's see, that was fourteen years ago, I went right to work climbing the corporate ladder. I wanted to have it all, you know what I'm saying—at least monetarily speaking. I was definitely a material girl. Had to have everything I saw. I was in love with words like *extravagant* and *lavish*, and I definitely followed their call."

I looked around at her brightly decorated living room.

"No, this is nothing," Ms. Race said, waving a piece of bread at it. "I mean, I had to have big, expensive furniture, all matching, and a new wardrobe every season. Some of the clothes I bought would hang in the closet with the tags still on them for months because I had so much stuff. And of course I drove a precious little sports car with leather interior. I just thought I was it on a stick."

She was talking as if she weren't too proud of all that. Personally, it sounded pretty good to me. For once though, I kept a lame thought to myself and filled my mouth with another spoonful of vegetable soup.

"I was going to be in debt forever. Within about a year all my credit cards were spent to the max, and I had to force myself to throw away all that mail that said, 'Your new, pre-approved credit card is waiting for your call!'" Ms. Race stirred her soup thoughtfully. "But who cared, you know? I had everything I wanted, so I figured it was worth it."

"Well yeah, I guess," I said.

She shook her head. "Not so. On those rare occasions when I was really honest with myself, I had to admit I still felt empty."

"Was that because you didn't have a boyfriend?" I said.

Her face crinkled all over. "I had those, too. Corporate executives love rich, classy women—or at least women who look like they are. No, I just had this big place inside me that all the dates and Armani shoes and RX-7s weren't going to fill up."

"So what happened?" I said. I was feeling eager for this to have a happy ending. "You're filled up now, aren't you? I mean, you seem like it."

"I definitely am and getting fuller all the time. But it didn't come easily. In fact, I fought it like somebody was trying to drag me into a concentration camp. I had this girlfriend I met at work. She was the receptionist, and I couldn't help but like her because her smile seemed so real. She didn't just turn it on as if she were flicking a switch the way everybody else did."

"Not you!"

"I was the worst. I had it down to a science. Anyway, her name was Donna, and we started having lunch together, chatting in the ladies' room, that kind of thing. One day I asked her if she wanted to go shopping on a Saturday with me, so we met at the mall. By the time we sat down to lunch, she looked as if she were in shock. She said, 'Enid, I have never seen anybody spend so much money on nothing in so short a time. You are amazing.'"

Ms. Race smiled, kind of shamefacedly. "I said to her, 'What do you mean "nothing"? That was all nice stuff!'

"Well, she didn't really answer me. She just said, 'You know, I'm going on a trip to Bolivia. It's a mission trip, but if you want to come with me, you don't have to do the mission work. You can just shop. You can find some great bargains down there!' That got my interest going, and since I'd pretty much exhausted all the good shopping in the States, I was ready to venture into foreign markets."

I looked around. "Is that where you bought all this neat stuff?"

"Wait; it's better than that," she said. "I took my vacation and went down there with Donna. The first couple of days I did the markets in the streets. They have all these people in their native Indian costumes with their booths on the sidewalk, and you can bargain with them." She scowled. "But on the second day, I was standing there trying to get this man with no front teeth and an obvious skin disease to give me a deal on a wallet I didn't need, when all of a sudden this little face peeked out from behind a stack of baskets. That was the cutest child I had ever seen. I squatted down to talk to him, and he came out—and I was appalled. That baby could barely walk, his little legs were so misshapen."

"Did he have some kind of disease, too?" I said.

"Malnutrition. We would all look like that if we didn't

have the proper food and medical care. I paid the guy full price for the wallet, and then I wandered the streets. I don't know how I'd missed it the first day—well, I do know. I was too busy looking for bargains, but the streets were literally filled with children like that—their noses all running, their eyes all hungry, their little bodies all malformed. Their parents looked even worse, even though they smiled and nodded. I couldn't figure out how they did it. I mean, overall the marketplace had this cheerful air about it like a festival was going on there in La Paz. But every individual vendor on that street had pain and suffering on his face or hers, and it was rooted in poverty."

She stopped to stare into her soup like she was seeing the whole thing being rerun right there. I put down my spoon. The story was making me feel guilty about eating.

"The third day I really started to study these people, and I noticed a lot of them were chewing on leaves. So I asked somebody who spoke English what they were. He explained to me that they were coca plants—"

"They make cocaine from them!"

"They do, but that takes a process. By themselves they don't give you a high or anything. These people were chewing on them because they kept the hunger pangs down." She sighed. "That did it for me. I changed all my paper money into coins, and I just handed them out to every mother and child who came up to me begging, and oh, they did, Cheyenne. It broke my heart.

"But that didn't even make a dent. I just felt so useless. When Donna came back to our room that night, I was lying facedown on the bed sobbing like a baby. She was wonderful. All she did was ask me if I wanted to go with her the next day. To tell you the truth, I only did it because I didn't want to go back out on the streets. She was so wise. She knew it was going to happen all along, but she just let me discover it for myself, and I tell you what, I did. It changed my whole life.

"I spent the next ten days helping to set up a children's

center—feeding little children, holding them while they got their shots, and teaching toddlers how to brush their teeth. We scrubbed floors, we handed out bread, we taught mothers what to do when their babies had diarrhea. We did it all. When we left, they were off to a good start, and I had basically given away everything I'd brought with me. Somewhere in Bolivia, a woman probably is still wearing a Versace scarf." She ran her finger around the edge of her pottery bowl. "As we were flying out of La Paz, I was feeling pretty good. You know, pretty smug. But when I looked at Bolivia below me, it hit me that there were still millions of people we didn't touch, and that was just Bolivia. What about Argentina? Ecuador? Peru? And how about Central America? Africa? All those Asian countries? Good grief, kids were starving right in the United States! I started to cry again. I was so overwhelmed."

"But you said you went back, like, every summer," I said. "Wasn't it hard, you know, because like you said, you hadn't even made a dent?"

"Not after Donna got through with me. No, I should say, not after God started on me. I said to Donna on the plane, 'I can't live the way I've been living. I'm going to give everything away, quit Dunn and Bradstreet, and join the Peace Corps.' Fortunately, she told me I ought to spend some time getting to know God first and finding out what He wanted me to do before I dumped my whole life. Now, as you yourself know, that was no easy task. Took me six months of really intense prayer and mentoring from her and some other people before I was even close to feeling like God would give me the time of day. But I became a Christian, and I started trying to model my life after Jesus' principles. I was on my way—and I made some remarkable discoveries."

"Like what?" I was totally into the story by then. My soup went cold in front of me.

"Like, first of all, I really didn't have to give away everything. Another Christian friend said, 'Look at all your desires, all the things you've always thought you wanted, and weed them out. Which ones can you live without and never give a second thought? Keep weeding until you get it down to the *holy* hungers.'"

I looked at my shirt again. "Like it says here."

"Right. She said those are the things you *should* have because God wants you to have them. Those you should keep and strive for. The rest can be used better by someone else." Ms. Race grinned now, like the ugly part of the story was over, and she had the right to be happy again. "I gave all my expensive furniture to a family whose house had just been destroyed by a fire. You talk about God—the timing was perfect. Then in my bare apartment, there were just all these big floor pillows I'd bought in Bolivia in these incredible colors."

"These," I said, pointing.

"Right. And a few pieces of pottery and some carvings. The place looked so empty, I moved into a smaller apartment!"

"What about your car?"

"Didn't need it in the city. I donated it to a Christian school for their driver's ed program. Kids have to learn to drive a stick shift, right?"

I was howling. "I'd love to go to that school!"

"It definitely drove up the enrollment in the class. When I came here, I needed a car so I bought Old *Señora*. She's a '93, but she's safe, and she gets me around."

"I think she's cool! I never saw a car that burnt orange color."

"I had it painted. That was a holy hunger. It reminds me of South America."

"Your clothes?"

"I gave most of the coats and sweaters to poor families. The business clothes I took to the Center for Abused Women. A lot of those women are trying to start over, but they've never worked in an office before, and they don't have the wardrobe."

"Didn't you need them for your job?"

"I kept the things I'd bought in South America. They didn't like that look much at Dunn and Bradstreet, but I wasn't long for the corporate world anyway. I asked God to send me where I was supposed to be. And a few weeks later a job came up for a secretary at a Christian school. Everybody said I was out of my mind, but I interviewed, they hired me, and I was in heaven. I knew within the first week that one of my holy hungers was kids, especially girls. I needed them in my life, and they needed me. One of the best parts of my job was that it left me free every summer. I started going on a two-month mission trip every year. I'd take things I didn't need anymore—stuff that just accumulates—to give away, and I'd come back with things I bought there to help the poor."

"That's where you got all your cool clothes and all this stuff here."

"Right. I do the same here in the U.S. I buy all my stationery from the Disabled Veterans, my books from the Salvation Army store, that kind of thing. It's kind of like my hobby, I guess."

"Your hunger."

"Exactly. I have a deep need to help people, and that means living my own life as simply as I can so I'm available to them. The result has been a life of abundance I never would have dreamed of."

"You don't seem that poor," I said.

"I'm not poor! All my hungers are satisfied. I have girls to minister to, great books to read, wonderful music to listen to. Those things allow me to serve God, rather than standing between us. And I have a really good time. I don't feel deprived—ever!"

It sounded so cool, I was ready to run right out and start giving things away.

Right.

Like what?

Ms. Race was watching me closely.

"What!" she said. "Those wheels are turning, and I don't think they're going in the right direction."

I shrugged, but I knew she wasn't going to be satisfied with that. And besides, I finally had somebody to listen to me. Why not just be honest? I had nothing to lose.

"You were rich to start with," I said. "I don't have anything, really. I can't even satisfy one holy hunger."

"You did it today," she said. "Didn't it feel good to serve those people?"

"*You* bought the food and everything."

"And you gave your jewelry to those little children."

"It was old, cheap stuff I made myself."

"And it was a thousand times more than what they already had. Besides, I told you, they appreciated the respect you showed them. That meant just as much as the food."

I studied my nub-nails. Ms. Race leaned over and lifted my chin with her fingertips. "Didn't you see the looks on the kids' faces when you gave them that necklace and those earrings?" she said. "I was watching. It was Christmas to them. They're going to be like that Bolivian woman with the Versace scarf. You give what you have, and your hunger starts to go away."

I still wasn't convinced. "But I don't even know what my holy hungers are. I try to listen to God. I do that thing of listening for ten minutes and then writing what I heard. Norie showed me. Sometimes it works, but lately . . ."

"Why don't you try a different approach?" Ms. Race said. "I think this might work better for you right now."

"What is it?" I said. I tried not to sound like I doubted it was going to work any better than my mother's waving her crystals around in her New Age phase.

"Start keeping a gratitude journal," she said. "Every night before you go to sleep write down five things you're grateful for, five different things every night. Then just before you close your eyes, say, 'Thank you, God.'"

"That's it?" I said.

"That's it. And I mean totally it. Don't pray *for* anything for a while."

"I thought we were supposed to take everything to God."

"We are, but . . . I can be perfectly honest with you, right?"

"Yeah," I said carefully. Honest, in my experience, usually meant I was about to be criticized.

"I've heard you pray, and I think it's wonderful that you're trusting God enough to at least say what you need. But praying isn't like writing a letter to Santa Claus. God knows what you need. So, for now, stop trying to *get* so you can feel God *give*."

I felt my face glowing hot with the shame thing. "I don't know if I can do that."

"And I'm positive that you *can*. Did you know that you and I are very much alike?"

"Us?! No way!"

"Sure. I still like those words *extravagant* and *lavish,* and so do you. And so does God. But—and this is a big one—just like I had to, you have to say thank you for what you already have. It's time you appreciated God's deep love."

I can't tell you how many times that sentence went through my head. Of all the things Ms. Race said to me that day, that was the one that stayed clearest. It was the one that made me rip a piece of paper out of my binder that night in my cave and number it one through five. It was the thing that forced me to stop thinking, "I'll never come up with five things" and just put the pencil tip on the page.

It was weird. What came to me right away was all the things that flashed in front of me when I was standing in the bead store waiting for Sam the Shop Sitter to call the cops. I started to write them down.

Tassie and our house.

Diesel and Felise.

Ms. Race.

Norie and the way she wouldn't let me fail in school.

Tobey and the way she was so careful not to hurt my feelings.

Brianna and the way she didn't care if she did hurt my feelings; she was going to get some sense into me.

And Marisa and Shannon and the way they were always so nice to me no matter how I messed up.

Fletcher. He had liked me for a couple of days. Shoot, that was like this gift or something. I hadn't felt so scraggly since then, come to think of it.

I was up to eight before I even knew it. Dude.

I folded the paper, put it under the cushion, and lay there with my eyes closed. My first impulse was to ask God for something—like don't let Tassie find out about the shoplifting, or don't let Fletcher find another girl too soon. But Ms. Race had said no. Besides, I was pleasantly sleepy. So much so that I conked out right there on the floor, still wearing my holy hungers T-shirt.

I didn't wake up until I heard Tassie outside my curtain the next morning. "Time to get ready for church, Cheyenne," she said.

I poked out a bed-head and grinned at her. I was actually smiling before I was even up.

"Okay," I said.

But my smile faded with her next two sentences. "I didn't mention this to you when you came in last night because you looked so happy. You got another letter from your mother yesterday."

CHAPTER THIRTEEN

"WHY?" I SAID.

I knew even then that I wasn't making sense, but it was all I could think of to say.

Tassie leaned her elbow on the bed above me and worked her lips like she was trying to get them going. "You won't know until you read her letter," she said finally. "But my guess is now that she's gettin' a clear head, she's missin' you."

"I don't think so!" I said. "You don't know her. She could care less about me, drunk or sober." I sat back on my feet and stared miserably at my bare knees. "And please don't say she's my mother so of course she cares. You never had to live with her."

"I wasn't going to say that," Tassie said. "All I was going to say was that you're right about the past. But none of us knows about the future—'cept the good Lord Himself."

She pulled an envelope out of the pocket of her robe. "Least you can do is read it."

I looked at the letter but didn't take it. "You're going to make me answer it, aren't you?"

"It would be the thing to do. But why don't you wait till the snake bites before you break out the anti-venom, Cheyenne."

I did feel like I was putting my hand out for a rattler, but I took the envelope.

"You still have time to read it and get ready for church,"

Tassie said. "And you won't want to miss breakfast. I made blueberry pancakes."

Those were my favorites. I looked up quickly, in time to see her eyes soften. She really did understand how hard this was.

When she left, I checked the room to be sure Felise and Ellie were both up and out of there. Ellie was probably standing in front of the mirror in the bathroom, judging from the pounding I could hear in the hall and the yelling from Avery. Felise was probably in the backyard. She liked to watch the sun come up in the winter when there was snow on the ground. Figure that out.

I pulled open the curtain so I could see and tore into the envelope. Maybe if I was really rough with it, I'd rip the letter, too, and wouldn't be able to read it.

No such luck. It came unfolded in one piece. I stared at the handwriting before I let any of the words sink in. It wasn't that sloppy. She was probably sober when she wrote it.

Big deal.

I procrastinated by smoothing it out on my lap, and then finally I read it, as fast as I could. But it wasn't fast enough to keep the bottom from dropping out of my world.

Dear Cheyenne Summer,

I know I haven't given you a chance to answer my last letter, but I have such exciting news, I had to write to you again.

They say here that I've been making such remarkable progress, I can have a pass. That means I get to leave the House and go out for two hours. Of course, the first thing I thought of was seeing you. It wouldn't be much. Maybe just an hour to have a Coke or something together.

Please write me back and tell me if you can meet me one of the next few Saturday afternoons. Then we can pick a place. You know Reno better than I do, I'm sure.

*I'm so excited I can hardly wait. I think this can be a
real start for us, Cheyenne.*

Love, Mama

I crumpled the paper into a ball in my hand. *A start? A
start to what? Four more miserable years with you before I can
legally escape on my own and never have to see you again?*

The paper ball went across the room, and I went back into
my cave where the cushion was waiting for my face.

"I can't do it!" I screamed into it. "I *won't* do it!"

But no matter how loud I hollered, I couldn't drown out
what the very thought of seeing my mother shoved into my
brain. If the best things in my life had flashed before my eyes
when I'd thought I was about to be arrested, the worst things
showed up now. It was an ugly vision I couldn't shut out, and
it was there in vivid detail.

What I saw went as far back as I could remember, before
our life turned black. There had been no father ever. Valerie,
my mother, never talked about him, even in those first years
in Elko, Nevada, where I was born. No pictures of him were
in our cabin in Winnemucca, in the shadow of the mountains, where we moved when I was about four.

I never remembered caring about having a father either. It
was enough just being her and me, I guess. Matter of fact,
they were the only good memories I had. But now they were
the ones that hurt the most, the ones I tried hardest to block
out.

She worked in an artists' co-op, making baskets and jewelry and pottery—stuff like that. She painted on cloth and all
that. She seemed big to me—everybody did—but I knew she
was tinier than the other women there. I thought she was so
beautiful, even down to the paint that was always under her
fingernails. She wore her hair, which had never been cut, in a
long braid down to her waist. I had to have mine like that,
too, and I said I'd never cut mine either, just to be like her.

I'd play while she was working. I liked the way tiny little

bubbles of sweat would come on her upper lip. I'd reach up and pop them with my fingers, and she would laugh. She had the biggest smile.

I never thought she was different from anybody else. I mean, I was four, five, six years old. What did I know about "normal"? Now I realized she was probably pretty bizarre.

She had found out we were part Native American right when I was born, so she went nuts over Washoe baskets and stuff. When I was about five, she got into making these wooden flutes and playing them and then sitting there for what seemed like hours with her eyes closed. We had crystals hanging everywhere during that phase, not to mention tarot cards.

Still, I thought I had everything. She would say to me while she was making a skirt or throwing a pot, "Cheyenne Summer, you watch the pieces that fall at my feet, and you dream. They'll become something special."

After a big pile of leftover cloth or a wad of unused clay collected, poof, the next day I'd have a doll or a set of dishes to play with. I think I was probably eight years old before I realized it wasn't from the magic of the Great Spirit.

I tried now not to think about the real magic of those years. The sunshine picnics on the desert under some tree that was the only one for miles. Playing with Mama's old paintbrushes, pretending they were my Indian people. Hearing her play the flute at night, or going with her to poetry readings outside and falling asleep and waking up with the stars twinkling over me.

Why would I want to shut it out? Because when I was seven, the door slammed closed on all that.

At some festival we went to, she met this man named Julius. I didn't like him from the start. You know how when you're little you can tell who's real and who isn't? He was the biggest fake since the Easter bunny, as far as I was concerned.

He probably wasn't that much older than my mother, but

he looked it to me because he had lost a lot of his hair. That wouldn't have been so bad, except that he grew what he did have really long, and it hung down in a ponytail to his waist. I didn't like it that he was copying Mama and me. Hey, I was just a kid.

But that wasn't it really. It was his eyes. They were small, and they always seemed to be moving. They weren't peaceful eyes. All the people I'd ever been around had peaceful eyes. The other thing was that when he smiled—and he was always plastering on this grin that looked like it belonged on some-body else's face—whenever he did that, I watched. I can stake my life on it—that smile never once reached his eyes. He was about the ugliest man I'd ever seen.

My mother didn't think so though. He stuck around when the festival was over, and it didn't seem like any time before he had moved in with us. I remember sticking really close to my mother those first few weeks and crying every time she went out of my sight. I'd do stuff, you know, like drop a bowl and let it break or go off too far on the desert without telling her, just to make sure she still noticed me. But all she could do was look at Julius.

One day they left me with a friend of ours, and when they came back and my mama was tucking me in bed, she told me they had gone to Reno to get married. He was my father now.

Once they were legal, he started acting like a father. Now after seeing Tobey's dad and even Norie's, I knew that wasn't the way all fathers acted. My mother had pretty much let me do my thing up until then, and mostly that had worked, I guess, because I didn't remember her yelling at me much. I didn't even know what being spanked or grounded was. But Julius had all these rules.

The problem was he didn't tell me what they were until I broke them, and then to be sure I never forgot, he beat them into me.

Like the first time I interrupted him when he was talking, he rapped me across the mouth. The first time I got out of bed to get a drink of water after Mama had tucked me in, he hit me seven times on the rear. One for each year of my age, he said.

I don't even want to tell you what happened the first time I had had enough and I yelled back at him.

It got so bad I started to wet the bed at night. If my mother didn't catch it and whip off the sheets before he got up, he would smack me silly. Then I'd hear him in their room, screaming at her for letting me be such a baby.

At first I thought she and I were just awful, rotten people since we couldn't seem to do anything right. After all, he was belting her, too.

But this one day—and I think now it was God's doing—I went to stay with our friend again while Mama and Julius—I refused to call him "Daddy"—went to Pyramid Lake to a storytelling thing. I wanted to go so bad, but Julius said since I hadn't cleaned up my room I wasn't worth taking. Anyway, at our friend's house—I can't even remember her name now—it was really hot, and she said I could play in this big washtub full of water she had in her backyard. I stripped down to my panties and jumped in. I was out there having probably the first good time I'd had since Julius showed up. She came running out the back door, and she just stood there staring at me. When I asked her what was wrong, she said, "Cheyenne, where did you get all those bruises?"

I looked down at myself, and I saw for the first time that I basically looked like a banana going bad. I guess I hadn't let myself notice before.

I really wanted to tell her. But I'd gotten so used to lying by then to save myself from beatings I told her I didn't know and that Julius said I was just a clumsy little ox and fell down all the time.

She didn't say anything then, but when she tucked me in that night, she said to me, "Cheyenne, I want you to know something. You are a good person. Don't let anyone ever tell you anything different."

Well, plenty of people had since then, and I'd let them. I mean, like I had a choice? But she must have planted a seed in me because, after that, every time Julius got in my face and started walin' on me, I'd say to myself, "You are a good person, Cheyenne."

I think that's when I started to hate my mother. She would try to cover up for me so Julius wouldn't find out I'd spilled a glass of milk or chewed my fingernails down to the nubs. But if he did find out and ripped off his belt, she would just stand there and not even try to stop him. I had the image burned in my brain like a brand on a steer of her standing in the doorway of my room with her arms folded across her chest and this blank glaze over her eyes while he whipped me, sometimes until I bled.

It got to the point, when I'd wake up at night and hear a chair break as he knocked her into it, I'd just scream into my pillow, "I don't care! I hate her!"

I was still too young to understand what was going on with her. I knew she smelled different now. I noticed that her hair was always kind of greasy like she never washed it. I saw that sometimes she acted as if she didn't understand me when I talked to her. She would take these really long naps in the middle of the day and let me start the dinner, which I never did right and always got smacked for.

Not until another kid at the artists' co-op teased me one day and said my mother was a drunk did I get it. Shortly after that she pretty much quit doing her art. That seemed to be okay with Julius. He was a painter, see, and he would out and out tell her she didn't have any talent. He was the one with the gift, and he didn't want her trying to show him up all the time with her pathetic attempts. The paint disappeared from under her fingernails.

Julius seemed to do pretty well selling his stuff, at least that was what I thought. He was all the time bringing home stereos and VCRs, and he had a new truck every six months. One night I did wonder when some guys came for supper, all the way from Ely, and I was sent to my room before it was even dark so they could talk business. I was still awake and watching out the window when they left at midnight. Nobody took a painting with him. The next day, Julius went out and bought this big leather couch that I wasn't allowed to sit on. It wasn't long before I knew about drug dealing, too.

If you're thinking I was living pretty high on the hog in those days, forget it. When Julius went off on his "painting trips" for a week or so at a time, I liked it because there was no hitting. But he wouldn't leave us with any food in the house, and my mother couldn't even grow vegetables anymore or go to the store. I actually ate a can of cold tomato paste one night because there wasn't anything else. As for clothes or toys, no way. My mother didn't sew for me anymore. Heck, she couldn't even make it to Kmart, much less paint a sunset on a dress like she used to. I hung onto one doll she had made me when I was little, although I had to keep it hidden because Julius had executed several on the kitchen table with a knife to teach me a lesson when I'd forgotten to feed the cat. But that one doll was it. When I was ten, I was still talking to her at night, telling her I was a good person.

Ten probably could have been a turning point for me. That was when I was attempting to cook spaghetti noodles one night, and Julius was screaming at me that I was stupid, stupid, stupid because they were sticking together, when the police came to the door. They knocked a couple of times and told Julius to open up. When he ran for the back bedroom, leaving me in the kitchen, right in the line of the front door, the cops busted it down and came in with their guns drawn. I don't mind telling you, I wet my pants.

One guy grabbed me and took me outside and sat with me in the backseat of his patrol car and gave me a peppermint from out of his pocket. It laid there in the bottom of my mouth while I watched the other policemen bring my mom and Julius out in handcuffs. I'm sure she didn't even know what was going on. She hadn't been out of bed for three days. But Julius was cussing and spitting and screaming about his rights. I only saw him once after that, and that was from behind about three sets of bars in the prison in Carson City. If anything, he had become even uglier.

But my life didn't improve a whole lot after that. They sent me to a foster home in Pahrump because my mother was in the women's prison after being convicted of drug charges, child negligence, and a bunch of stuff I'd known but had never put names to. At the foster home, the only good thing I can say is that I had three meals a day.

That's when, at age ten, I also started school. You talk about a miserable experience. I knew nothing about sitting in a desk, listening to a teacher. Words on a page might as well have been written in Japanese. And math, dude, I didn't even have a clue to addition. Forget subtraction or multiplication. About the time I was supposed to start school my mother had been in her learn-from-Mother-Earth phase. I could have told you every plant that grew in Nevada, but I didn't even know it was a state. What was a state?

Two other kids lived in that home. They were both girls who were about eleven. They were sisters, twins in fact, and they were geniuses at finding things to do for fun in the deathly boring town of Pahrump.

Lark and Starling—what was up with these parents and their nature names?—thought I was weird from the start. So to fit in, I did whatever they came up with. Otherwise, I'd have been so lonely I probably would have died right there.

When they figured out whose houses were open during the day while people were out, they would let themselves in to ransack the places. I was with them. We didn't take too much, at least I didn't, but we played pranks like unrolling the toilet paper and putting Vaseline on the doorknobs.

But Lark and Star weren't as smart as they thought they were, and I never claimed to be, so we eventually got caught. Our foster "parents" wanted to get rid of all three of us; so the state shipped me off to a different foster home in Beowawe. I don't even count that one. There weren't any other kids in the house. The people were way old, and they couldn't hear me when I talked half the time. I just couldn't stand the silence. You know, not being heard, not being talked to. I even imagined that the doll wasn't listening anymore, and I tore her apart. I felt like I was in a bad dream all the time. One day when I was supposed to walk to school, I just took off.

I hitched a ride with some teenagers who I think were also on the lam and spent two days riding around with them. They were cool enough to feed me beef jerky and Cheetos, but not cool enough to grab me and stuff me in the car when the cops showed up at a mini-mart we were at. The teenagers squealed out of there and left me doing wishful thinking in front of the candy counter. The guy at the cash register pointed me out to the police, and they hauled me off to the juvenile shelter.

Since foster care wasn't my thing, I started going down the ladder of options. They told me my mother was to be released from prison in six weeks. I was now almost twelve. So they put me in a temporary group home in Yerington.

They had about as many rules there as Julius did. Of course, theirs made sense, and they didn't knock your teeth out when you messed up. But by then, I didn't know how to be anything but this major manipulator. I lied about everything, just because the truth had always gotten me in trouble. I stole stuff from the other kids because I knew I was never going to get anything otherwise. Then I smiled at everybody and talked their ears off because silence scared me so much. I'm pretty sure they were glad to see me go.

I wasn't. Even there, or any of the foster homes I'd been in, would have been better than the next two years with my mother. Pardon my language, but it was pure, well, Hades.

Valerie was dry while she was in prison—like she had access to gin and tonic there, right? But the minute she was released, and we were living in Elko where she told the authorities she had family—one sister who didn't speak to her anymore—anyway, I'd barely put my two pairs of jeans into the drawer in this awful little rented house before she was downing a bottle of cheap wine. She said she was celebrating her new job at a video store.

She worked mostly evenings. And she almost always came home drunk. I knew what it was about now—the slurred speech; the bloodshot, baggy eyes; the puffed-up face. But I found myself wishing she was the same kind of drunk she had been before—just go to bed and sleep for days or sit there staring into space. Prison must have done something to her because now she was a mean drunk. She would come in from work, stand over my bed, and yell at me for not cleaning the house or having her supper ready. Like there was anything to clean or make supper with.

I started to hang out at the 7-Eleven with the high school kids because they always had junk food they were willing to share. They weren't stingy with the pot and beer, either, both of which kept me from noticing I didn't have decent clothes or school supplies—my two biggest reasons for cutting classes.

When the school finally reached my mother at work—at the beginning of her shift so she was basically coherent—she decided she had to go off booze and straighten me out. Of course, the only methods she knew she had learned from Julius. Matter of fact, she decided then she should try to get back with him because at least he had made me behave. She borrowed some guy's car, and we drove all the way to Carson City to visit Julius on a Sunday. I refused to speak to him, and he didn't seem too enthusiastic about getting back together with Valerie either.

She started to drink as soon as we got home. I just couldn't take it. I hated her. I hated my life. I basically hated myself. I didn't even grab what few things I had. I just left the next night when she went to work. I started to walk. Nobody picked me up this time. I was about half-dead two days later, staggering around who knows where, when the highway patrol found me.

I spent a couple of days in the hospital, and the next six months in Wittenberg. That's supposed to be a junior rehab thing where "troubled" kids get a dose of reality and either get straight or go on down the tubes. They told me my mother was in intensive rehab and was getting herself together, and I ought to try to do the same.

I guess I tried. I was scared enough. Those girls in there—they were what Tassie called "hard core." Brick walls are softer. Most had snorted, shot up, and inhaled any illegal substance you could name. And I thought Julius was mean? I'd have loved to have set a couple of those girls on him when he was unarmed. They could make a weapon out of anything. Like, I woke up one night, and this girl was poking me with a paper clip, just for grins.

So, yeah, I did what I could to straighten up. The people there didn't help me that much. The only one who ever helped was that friend back in Winnemucca telling me I was a good person. I didn't believe it, but I just kept saying it to myself over and over. If I was ever going to accept it, I decided I was going to have to be as different from my mother as I could. At dinner one night, I got a hold of a knife somebody had carelessly left unguarded on the serving line and went into the bathroom and whacked off my hair.

I also stopped cussing because my mother cussed. I made a vow never to drink or use drugs because she did. I even started trying in class since she hadn't made me go to school. That didn't get me too far. I figured I was just stupid. Good, but stupid. You can't win them all.

They finally decided I was ready to try foster care again. They were smart enough to send me someplace I'd never lived before so I didn't have a reputation to live up to. They picked Lovelock.

It had all the signs of being another dead end. The school

didn't know what to do with me because I was so far behind. I didn't fit in with any of the kids because I wore lame clothes and now had this perpetual bad-hair day. Plus I tended to explode when I became frustrated, which didn't exactly win me any friends.

But two things saved me. One was that although the lady I was living with acted like she was scared of me, she was the crafts type, and she had a whole roomful of nothing but art supplies. Although I had vowed to be different from my mother, I couldn't stay out of that room. I don't think I was even remembering my mother when I was drawn to the beads. My foster "mother" said I could have all I wanted—as long as I stayed out of trouble.

I started to make necklaces and earrings, and I experimented with different combinations on bracelets, anklets, and little toe rings. I'd wear them to school and other girls would actually say, "Those are neat." Of course, when I said I'd made them, they said, "No way," which wasn't exactly a compliment, but it had me making piles of jewelry and wearing something different every day. I'd also carry some in my pocket for bribery purposes.

Somebody would say, "Hey, those are cool," and I'd say, "I'll give you a pair if I can go skating with you guys tonight." What did they care? They were happy to get me in—and then dump me—so they could have a rad loop of beads hanging from their earlobe.

That's how I found the other thing I had going for me. I was standing out behind the skating rink one night. I'd followed some kids back there because I was about to die of loneliness. This guy looked at me twice, which nobody hardly ever did, and offered me a puff of his cigarette. I was about to take it in spite of my anti-mother vow, when this car drove up, spraying gravel all over the place.

Everybody else scattered, but I was a little slow. I mean, it wasn't a police car so what was the big deal? I guess they all thought it was a plain-clothes cop or something. Turns out, the guy who leaned out the window and said, "Honey, thank the Lord, I thought you were going to take a drag off that cigarette," was the priest at the Episcopal church.

I didn't know that right away, of course. He didn't ask me to get in the car with him. He didn't even get out. He just talked to me for a while, gave me his card, and said next time I was tempted to do something stupid to just call him, day or night, and he would come help me.

I still thought it was some kind of setup. He had to be a child molester, right? You can't blame me for thinking that after all I'd been through. But I guess I didn't really believe it because about a week later I was walking out of the school building when these three girls came up to me and told me if I didn't stop trying to buy my way into their group, they were going to beat me up, just jump me when I least expected it.

I said I got it. Then as I walked away, I started to shake. I knew if I just went home, I'd go into the bathroom, take a razor, and slit my wrists. And I knew I didn't want to do it.

Instead, I went back in the school building, and I grabbed the phone when the secretary was turned the other way—because they wouldn't let you use it and I didn't have a quarter for a pay phone—and I called Father Dale. He was there in, like, five minutes, and I was waiting for him on the front steps of the school. I didn't even care if he was a child molester. At least he had acted like he wanted to be around me.

We went by my foster mother's work, and he asked if I could come to dinner at his house. He and his wife bought a pizza, and all three of us sat around while I told them my story. I sobbed all these tears I'd been storing up since I was about ten. I fell asleep crying on their couch.

When I woke up the next morning, Father Dale was sitting there in the same clothes he had had on the night before. He had stayed there all night, I guess. He asked me if I was ready to turn my whole, horrible life around. What else was I going to say? I said yes. He prayed with me—now that was a new experience—and then he said he was going to get to work on it. Meanwhile his wife would tutor me at their house so I didn't have to put up with those kids, and he would take care of it with the school.

In a couple of days, I moved in with them, although they told me it was only temporary. The real place I should be, he said, was with a woman in Reno named Tassie McBrien. I told him I'd do anything as long as she would halfway care about me. He said she would care about me 100 percent.

I pulled myself up off the cushion now and realized I was sobbing again, just like I had that night at Father Dale's. I really had turned my life around. Ms. Race was right. I already had everything—in abundance, like she said. I knew it now. Why would I want to take a chance on messing that up?

I wiped my nose with the back of my arm and scrambled around for my binder. The paper tore when I ripped it out, but I didn't care. Snatching up my pen, I wrote a letter to my mother.

> *Dear Valerie,* (it said)
>   *It sounds like things are going better for you. That's good. They're going better for me, too. That's why I just don't see the point in us meeting. I don't think it would work for me to ever come live with you again.*
>   *Good luck.*
>
>   *Cheyenne*

That lady way back in Winnemucca may have been right. I scratched out *Good luck* and wrote *God bless you*.

Weird though. As right as it seemed, I didn't feel any freer when I folded up the letter and went out in the living room to look for an envelope.

TASSIE SAID WE WERE GOING TO BE LATE FOR church and to just leave the envelope on her shelf. She would mail it later. I threw on some clothes, sat through church like a zombie, and picked at my fried chicken and mashed potatoes at Sunday dinner. I figured maybe if I stayed numb long enough, my doubts would go away and I could go back to "good" and "grateful" and all those things I'd had a chance to enjoy for all of about twelve hours.

I was managing with the numb thing pretty well until after dinner when Norie came over to tutor me. Tassie told Felise and Ellie they were all going to Costco to buy food for the month, and she said Avery and Brendan had to go, too.

"Man, no way!" Avery said, straining his sore-throat voice. "What am I going to do, stand around with my thumb in my mouth?"

Brendan, of course, nodded that he, too, was indignant.

"No," Tassie said. She wasn't even raising her voice as she put on her coat. "You're going to do two things. You're going to help with the carts, and you're going to speak to me with respect."

The voice went up. "What did I say? Man, I can't even open my mouth around here anymore without gettin' busted."

"You aren't busted—yet." Tassie steered him toward the door.

"I was going to skateboard. Me and Brendan both were."

"You *were,*" she said, "till I got word you two might be doing a little more than skatin' back there behind Safeway. That wouldn't be music to your probation officer's ears, Avery. I want to be able to give him a good report on you when I see him."

"He's a pig," Avery said.

Thankfully, the door closed behind them then.

But Tassie opened it a crack again and said, "This way you can have some quiet to concentrate. If you need anything, Diesel's out here working on his truck."

Norie and I parked in the living room in front of the fireplace. I plopped on one of the red corduroy love seats, and she stretched out on another.

"You ready to whip through those vocabulary words?" she said.

I nodded.

"You got the list?"

I nodded again and pawed through my backpack.

"You want to start with me calling them out to see how many you already know?"

Another nod from me.

Norie didn't say anything. I looked up at her. She was staring me down with this look that always reminded me of two syringes coming at me.

"What?" I said.

"Talkative today, aren't you?"

"No," I said. "Just call out the words, okay?"

"No."

"Then I'm going to flunk."

"Knock it off, Cheyenne," Norie said.

She sat up straight on the love seat and pushed her hands through her hair like two rakes. "You're pulling that I-don't-want-to-talk-about-it thing again. Come on, it's me. Don't be—"

"What?" I said. "Stupid? Is that what you were going to

say? Why don't you just go ahead? Call me an idiot because I
don't talk about my problems, even though nobody can do
anything about them anyway! Ms. Race tried, you guys tried,
but it doesn't matter because my mother is the one who's stupid. No matter what, I can't get away from her—and when I'm
with her I'm just like her, so why doesn't everybody just leave
me alone and let me hate her!"

I knew I was screaming, but I must have been louder—
and more hysterical—than even I knew. Norie was standing
up, and her face was draining. The front door flew open, and
Diesel stomped in with a wrench still in his hand. I think he
thought somebody was attacking me, the way he was waving
it around.

Me, I was charging around the room, hurling pillows and
slamming my fist into walls and waiting for my chest to explode. Until Diesel grabbed me from behind, greasy hands
and all, and Norie walked toward me like I was a dog she
hoped had had its rabies shots.

"Chey, chill, okay?" she said. Her voice was shaky. You
didn't hear it like that often.

"I was trying to chill, and you told me not to!" I shouted
at her. I was crying now, which somehow gave me permission
not to make any sense.

"If I let go of you, are you going to sit down, or are you
going to keep tearin' the house apart?" Diesel said behind me.

"I don't know!" I blubbered.

Norie nodded to him, and his hands went slack. I rushed
forward, straight into Norie's arms. She hugged me so hard
I couldn't have gotten away if I'd wanted to. And I didn't
want to.

"I haven't seen her carry on like this since she first got
here," Diesel said as Norie led me to a love seat and sat down
with me.

"This was a frequent occurrence?" Norie said.

"About once a day the first couple of weeks."

"Would you quit talking about me like I'm not here!" I said through my sobs.

"Then listen to me," Norie said. Her voice was strong again. She pulled me away from her and held me at arm's length so I had to look at her. "I thought everything was okay now that the shoplifting thing was over."

"I thought so, too! But now my mother wants to see me—and she can because she's in this halfway house, and they're going to let her out for a couple of hours, and she wants me to meet her, and I don't want to! I can't, Norie!"

I started to lose it again. She said the only thing she could have said to make me calm down. "Okay, Chey," she said. "Just hang in there. We'll have a Flagpole meeting."

"Can we?" I said. "Do you think the Girls could help with this?"

"We'll just meet, and we'll take it from there. We've never let you down, have we?"

I shook my head. Out of the corner of my eye, I could see Diesel picking up pillows and looking pretty relieved.

"I'll get everybody together tomorrow at lunch," Norie said.

"But one thing," I said suddenly.

"What?"

"No Fletcher. I don't want him to know anything about this."

She looked at me for a second while she chewed on her lip. But then she said, "Okay. It'll be just us girls. Diesel, would you—"

"I know the drill," he said. "Man, I gotta eat lunch with that kid again?"

I'd have killed to eat lunch with Fletcher. But that fell into the no-sense-even-thinking-about-it category. It was enough just then to know the Girls could help me. My mind started to come unjumbled. Norie and I actually got some studying done.

And that night, when I was lying in bed, I even remembered I was supposed to write in the gratitude journal. Amazing, considering that Tassie was down the hall in Avery's room trying to talk to him, while he was yelling his head off at her. I shut them out and crawled down into the cave.

"Tassie says you have to sleep in your bed tonight," Ellie muttered from hers. "She says we can't afford a chiropractor for you."

"Shut up," I said.

"No dessert," Felise mumbled.

I ripped out a piece of paper, but for a while I could only stare at it. I'd already written about the only things I figured I had to be thankful for, and Ms. Race said it had to be five different things every night. I closed my eyes and thought back over the day.

Diesel's not telling Tassie I'd had a tantrum and tried to trash the house, that was definitely one. Tassie making my favorite breakfast because she knew I was going to have a hard day. Yeah. The meeting to look forward to. Norie hugging me even though I knew she wasn't that wild about hugging.

I needed one more.

"You better get in your bed, or you'll be grounded for life," Ellie hissed from above.

A bed to sleep in. I was pretty sure those little kids I'd given the beads to didn't have one.

That was five. As I folded the list and put it with the other one under my cushion, I reminded myself not to pray, "God, let something happen so I don't have to see my mother." I whispered instead, "Thank you, God."

"Would you hush up?" Ellie said. "Some of us are tryin' to sleep."

"G'night, Ellie," I said, as I climbed up into my bed.

"You are so weird," she said.

I was actually feeling ready for the day the next morning when I dumped my backpack by the front door and went into the kitchen for the required bowl of oatmeal. This time the feeling lasted for about a minute.

"Take your time, Cheyenne," Tassie said to me as I glanced up at the clock. "I'm driving you to school today."

"How come she's getting all these rides lately?" Ellie said. "What about me?"

"You can take the bus," Tassie said. "Cheyenne might be late."

"I guess if you want privileges around here you have to be a psycho," Ellie said, as she stabbed her hands into the sleeves of her jacket. "I'm going to start acting weird."

"Too late," Avery said.

He dodged her punch and went for the door.

"Avery," Tassie said.

It was Brendan who stopped, tugging on his earring. Avery didn't even look at her. "I'm going to pick up your progress report at school, and then I'm going to see your probation officer today."

"I didn't do anything this weekend," Avery said sullenly.

"I know. But what about this attitude?"

Avery shook his head so his hair went into his eyes. "What attitude?"

I didn't listen to the rest. I suddenly went cold. Why was Tassie taking me to school—late, too? She had this thing about us getting ourselves there, and on time. This could only mean bad news.

This could only be my mother.

Is she coming over here for breakfast? Is Tassie going to tell me to pack my bags? Am I ever going to see the Girls again?

Okay, so I was going a little psycho like Ellie said. Can you blame me?

Tassie waited until everyone was out the door before she sat down at the table with me. I pushed my oatmeal bowl away. There was no way any cereal was going down. I could barely swallow.

"Don't beat around the bush, okay?" I said. "It's about my mother, isn't it?"

Tassie raised an eyebrow. "Well, now, you got right to the point, didn't you? I'm glad to see it for a change. No sense hiding from the truth."

"What is the truth?" I said. "Just tell me."

Tassie reached in her pocket and brought out my letter, which I'd left on the shelf for her to mail. It wasn't in an envelope. "I don't know if you remember the regulation," she said. "It's one I hate, but I do it because I try to follow the rules."

"What regulation?"

"The one that says I have to read your outgoing mail. Like I said, I hate it, because I trust you."

"It's okay if you read that," I said. "I didn't say anything bad in there."

"No, matter of fact, you were real up-front. You have to be if you and your mother are ever going to see eye to eye again."

"What difference does it make?" I said as I tried to memorize the figures on the tablecloth. "I don't ever want to see her again."

Tassie crossed her arms on the table and leaned forward on them, boring her eyes into me until I looked straight at her.

"Cheyenne," she said, "you might not have any choice but to see your mother. The judge has the final word—and if she says you have to give it a go, you have to give it a go."

I could have said all kinds of things, things like: "That judge can go suck an egg as far as I'm concerned; I'm not seeing her!" or "I'll see her if they force me, but I don't have to talk to her. They can't make me talk!"

But the loudest thing in my head was Norie's voice, weird as that may sound. I could just hear her saying, "We'll have a Flagpole meeting. We've never let you down, have we?"

No, they hadn't. They were going to make this okay, just like they had with the lady in the bead store. The judge could say whatever she wanted to, but nobody was stronger than my Girls when they got together with God. There was just no point in discussing this with Tassie.

I pulled off a pretty convincing shrug. "I guess I'll do whatever I have to," I said. "Go ahead and mail that anyway, would you?"

Tassie blinked.

"Okay?" I said. "I really have to get to school. I have a vocabulary test first period."

"Okay," Tassie said. She blinked again, and then she got up and put on her coat.

I actually did pretty well on the test, thanks to Norie.

I outran everybody in PE, too, and stayed awake all through my special reading class. I had the meeting to cling to, and it made all the difference.

The only rough spot was Spanish because Fletcher was in there. I expected him to be flirting with every other little *señorita* now that he had gotten the hint I wasn't available. But he didn't poke anybody with a pencil, steal anybody's binder, or any of his usual "pre-dating rituals," as Tobey called them. Part of me was glad to see that, but part of me knew it really didn't matter. I couldn't have him; so why even think about it?

Right. It was kind of like telling yourself not to think about apples. Your mind is suddenly crammed with sauce, pies, and candied apples on a stick.

But lunchtime finally arrived, and I mowed down half a dozen people getting to the theater lobby.

"Hey, no running in these halls!" Mr. Dixon, one of the math biggies, called out to me from somewhere in the crowd.

"I'll take care of her," someone else said.

I grinned. It was Ms. Race, who took me by the shoulder, crinkled her eyes down at me, and said, "Need an escort, Ernie Irvin?"

"Who's Ernie Irvin?" I said.

To my horror, a voice behind us said, "He's a race car driver. I like Mark Martin myself. Where you guys going?"

It was Fletcher, tagging along behind us like a Labrador puppy. An adorable Labrador puppy.

I wanted to bolt. Only because Ms. Race hadn't let go of me did I keep walking casually.

"We're going to do girl talk," Ms. Race said. "Now unless you've done something drastic, Fletcher, I think that disqualifies you."

"Man, this is so unfair!" he said. "This is the second meeting you guys have had without us. I thought this was supposed to be like a Christian group—not the Garden Club or something."

"Nobody's keeping you fellas from doing your own thing." Ms. Race winked at me. "Or can't you get it together to pray without the women?"

Fletcher gave another "Aw, man!"

Now, mind you, all this time he never cast an eye in my direction. The whole conversation was carried on with Ms. Race. But when Diesel appeared and hauled Fletcher out of the mob, Ms. Race squeezed my shoulder, let go, and said, "Since when was Fletcher so into prayer?"

"I don't know," I said.

"You do, too. That boy is smitten if I ever saw it."

"What's 'smitten'?" I said.

"Who's smitten?" That was Shannon, who caught up with us and linked her arm through mine. "We just had that on a Shakespeare vocabulary list in English. There was a bunch of weird stuff on there: 'forsooth,' 'withal.'" She gave my elbow a gentle jerk. "So who's smitten?"

"What's it mean?"

"It's when somebody thinks somebody else is hot," she said.

"Oh," I said. "Nobody's 'smitten.'"

I stopped myself from thinking it would be neat if Ms.

Race were right, and I sat down in my usual spot in the circle. Everybody was there within minutes, and I made a note to myself to write that in my gratitude journal that night—along with what was about to happen, of course. I didn't know how they were going to find a way to get me out of this thing with my mother, but just knowing they would kept my chest from hurting for about the first time in twenty-four hours.

"Hey," Tobey said, nudging me and grinning her wonderful smile, "I thought we were done with you. Here you are back again with *another* problem!"

"I think this one's tougher," Norie said. "We're going to need some major prayer."

"Spill it," Brianna said. "I've been dyin' of curiosity all morning."

I spilled it, though with a lot less drama than I'd told it to Norie. It helps when you're not blubbering all over yourself. They all watched me with their beautiful, concerned eyes, and everybody kept nodding. When I was done, I already felt better, and nobody had even made the first suggestion for a Plan of Action yet.

There was a long silence. Brianna was the first one to speak.

"Let me get this straight," she said. "Your mother is gettin' her life together, and part of that for her is seein' you. Only she's been such a—"

"Shrew," Shannon put in quickly. She looked around at us. "That was on our Shakespeare list, too."

"Right. She's been such a 'shrew' to you, you don't want to see her."

"That's an understatement," Norie said.

There was another silence. This one made me a little uneasy.

"You get it, don't you?" I said. "Tassie says if the judge says I have to see her, I have to. But that can't happen. I can't see her. Not now when everything is finally going right for me."

Marissa looked nervous, glancing from person to person in the circle. I still didn't think too much of it. Marissa always looked nervous.

"I may be dense," she said, "but exactly what is it you want us to do, Cheyenne?"

I sighed patiently. "I need you to help me find a way so I don't have to meet with her."

"Oh," Tobey said. "Uh, okay."

"What okay?" Brianna was sitting straight up, hands spread out in midair, eyes blazing. Her gold hoop earrings were swinging like an earthquake was going on inside her head. She leaned in toward me, and I actually felt a pang of fear go through me, she was so intense. "You just want to run away from this, don't you, girl?" she said. "Well, if you do, don't count on me to help you!"

CHAPTER FIFTEEN

I COULDN'T CLOSE MY MOUTH, NOT UNTIL SHANNON reached over and touched my arm. I shook off her hand and got up on my knees.

"I don't understand," I said. "I thought you were going to help me!" I glanced wildly at Ms. Race. "This is my holy hunger—never to have to deal with my mother again and to stay at Tassie's! I'm being grateful. So why can't I ask for that?"

Everybody in the circle looked as if she would rather be anywhere else. No one seemed to want to meet my eyes. I looked at Ms. Race again, but she didn't say a word. Instead, Brianna spoke, and just then I'd rather have heard from just about anybody else. "You can't ask God for something that isn't good for you, Cheyenne," she said. "And running away isn't good for you."

"You haven't lived my life. How do you know?"

Brianna bunched up her lips for a second. "Because it isn't what Jesus would do—and that's what we always try to figure out here, right? When we make a Plan of Action, it's what we think Jesus would do. You can't just ask the Lord to do it your way. You have to do it His way."

My eyes went to Norie, but she was nodding like Brianna had just preached another Sermon on the Mount.

Even Tobey seemed to agree with her, the way she was fiddling with her necklace and looking as if she were picking out words for me. "It seems like you have to at least give your mom a chance. Nobody's going to make you live with her the first time you meet. So why not—"

I didn't hear the rest. I'd already heard enough. Right there, in the midst of the Flagpole meeting, my old self kicked back in. Brianna was right; I wanted to run.

And I did.

I couldn't even see as I flailed my way across the theater lobby and blew through the double doors. On the other side, I plowed right into Fletcher and fell headlong to the floor. I could feel the carpet burning my hands as I skidded to a stop.

"Whoa!" Fletcher said.

He stuck out his hand, I guess to help me up, but I smacked it away and scrambled to my feet on my own. He was standing right in my way though. I'd have had to shove him against the wall to get past him, and I was running out of steam.

"I thought you guys were having a girl meeting," he said. "Did somebody say something to tick you off?"

I slapped at my face to get the stubborn tears off. "I thought I had friends!" I shrieked at him. "But I don't have anybody! I'm just as alone as I ever was!"

He just stood there, looking at me. He wasn't going to move. Ready to tear my own hair out by the roots, I turned around the other way and shot back toward the double doors.

"Where do you think you're going?" somebody yelled behind us.

Good grief, was there no end? It was Mr. Dixon again.

"You're not allowed in that lobby during lunch!" he barked at me.

"She's at a meeting," Fletcher said.

"Doesn't look like it to me. Back this way, young lady."

With a wave of his arm, he ushered me toward the front of the school. As soon as I heard him yelp at somebody else, "What are you doing with that soda can in these halls," I made a blind dash for the front door. Cold air blasted my face, but my cheeks were so hot—from tears, from anger, from absolute frustration—it might have felt good to me, if anything in the world could feel good at that point. The sun bit at the edges of the afternoon, but it was a black day as far as I was concerned. And a black life. I was going right back where I'd struggled so hard to come from.

A horn blew, and I realized I was at the street. I let the car pass and then just kept running. I smelled cigarette smoke and onions, and I heard somebody say, "Did you finally freak out?"

That same somebody grabbed my arm, and I looked straight into Avery's sharp little yellow-brown eyes.

"Hey, stand right there!" somebody else said, laughing harshly. "You're breakin' the wind. Just stand there till I get this lit."

I glanced over my shoulder where a guy in a black Raiders hat was putting a match to a cigarette with chapped hands. He looked up at me with a dry smile and said, "Thanks."

I caught my breath and yanked my arm away from Avery.

"What are you havin' a breakdown over this time?" he said.

"I'm not having a breakdown," I said.

I looked around at the little bunches of people who were sharing cigarettes, private jokes, and a couple of sandwiches from Port of Subs. I was in the middle of the Don't Give a Hang gang.

"Coulda fooled me," Avery said. He nodded at Brendan who had somehow appeared beside him. Like always, Brendan just nodded back and stuck his hands in his pockets. He was the only one there who looked like he was cold, or at least the only one who would admit it. Everybody else looked too hard to feel anything.

"I'm mad," I said. "Aren't I allowed to get mad? And don't say it's PMS, or I'll pound you."

"Hey, it didn't even enter my mind," Avery said. His eyes

shifted, and out of the corner of his mouth, he said to Brendan, "It's PMS."

I didn't even try to punch him. Who cared? It wasn't going to get me anywhere. Nothing was going to get me anywhere, not as long as my mother kept barging in to ruin my life. Not as long as I didn't have any control.

"Look out, she's gonna blow," Avery said. He took a step back, pretending to duck an approaching grenade or something. I just stood there.

Avery squinted at me. "What's goin' on?" he said. "You on somethin'?"

"No!"

"Maybe you oughta be." He nudged Brendan and raised his voice. "Hey, anybody got any—"

"Shut up," I said. "I don't want drugs. I just want . . ."

I stopped.

"What?" he said.

I pulled my arms up into my sweater sleeves. I hadn't even grabbed my coat out of my locker. It had to be twenty degrees out here, colder with the wind hitting us.

"I don't know. Maybe I want out of this state. Someplace where my mother can't find me. I don't know. I'm just talking stupid. I have to go to class."

I started for the street, but Avery grabbed my arm again.

"Are you thinkin' of runnin'?" he said.

"No," I said. "I told you, I was just talkin' stupid."

Avery looked at Brendan, and then he came really close to me, so close I could see the little yellow places between his crooked two front teeth. I backed up a step.

"What?" I said.

"What's goin' on?" he said. "You're actin' like you're autistic or somethin'. It's creepin' me out. Come on, we ain't gonna tell anybody."

On cue, Brendan shook his head. Normally, I would have been waiting for Avery's punch line. But he looked like he actually wanted to know.

"They're making me meet with my mother—probably," I said. "And I can't. She'll mess everything up. She'll mess *me* up. I thought my friends would help me, but they think I should do it."

Avery rolled his eyes. "Right, and how many of them have parents that have ever slapped the snot out of them?"

I looked at him sharply. "Who told you about my mom?"

"Nobody. But why else would you be in a foster home? I mean, come on. We've all been there."

"Yeah," Brendan said.

Avery nodded. "My old man used to get so wasted he would throw furniture at me. The state took me away when he hit me with the microwave."

"You're lying," I said.

"Okay, don't believe me—nobody does. But I know where you're comin' from. You just get so sick of people who don't know beans about your life tellin' you how to live it—right?"

I nodded. I was too stunned to do anything else. Avery was almost making sense.

"Here, wipe your nose," he said. He handed me a Port of Subs napkin, and I got rid of the snot and the tears while he dug his hands into his sweatshirt pockets. His face was serious. He looked a lot older when he wasn't smirking like a convict.

"Don't do it," he said abruptly. "Don't meet your old lady. If she messed you up before, she'll mess you up again. You'd be better off running away."

"I did that a couple of times," I said. "It didn't work."

"How old were you? Ten? Twelve? Give me a break. You could make it now."

"Right. Whatever." My chest was starting to tighten.

"I'll even go with you. So will Brendan. We've just been waitin' for a chance."

"Why?" I said. "Are they trying to make you go back to your dad?"

"No, but I've had it with Tassie bein' on my case. I figure I've done better here than I have anyplace, and it still isn't good enough. I just want to do what I want. Point is, we basically got our stuff together now. We oughta just blow—the three of us—four of us."

"What four?" I said.

Avery nodded toward the guy with the dried out smile who was finishing his cigarette.

"Who's that?" I said.

"He doesn't go here. He dropped out. But he'll give us a ride anywhere—he told us that." Avery spat on the frozen ground and stretched his face out of the hood of his sweatshirt. "Hey, Kenny."

"What?"

"If we wanna split, can you take us to like Sacramento or somewhere?"

"Who?"

"Me and Brendan and her."

Kenny ran his murky eyes over me and shrugged. "Sure. When you wanna go?"

Avery looked at me. "Let's just go now. Tassie's out—I know 'cause she's over talkin' to my probation officer. We just go home, grab our stuff, and bail. You think?"

No, I did not think—about anything. My head was frozen, and not from the cold.

Brendan didn't look much more enthusiastic than I was, but of course, when Avery looked at him, he nodded, shrugged, and sniffed.

Dude, they really didn't care about anything over here on this side of the street. You want to run off to Sacramento? Sure, let me just finish this cigarette, then I'll help you . . .

Help me what? Throw away my life?

Where had I heard that before? It took me about two seconds to remember. Elena. Angel Lady. She had said not to throw away my chances. She had been so nice to me. Ms. Race had been so nice to me, telling me, "It's time you appreciated

God's deep love." The Girls had been good. They had helped me confess. And Tassie—she made me blueberry pancakes . . .

"Look, if you're gonna cry, forget it," Avery said. "I'm going anyway. It's in my head now; I gotta do it." He nodded to Brendan and Kenny, and the three of them started off toward the curb. Avery glanced over his shoulder without really meeting my eyes.

"You comin' or not?" he said. "If you're not, you better not let Tassie catch you over here."

Or Brianna, I thought.

But Brianna couldn't help me. None of them could. Or would. So far Avery had offered the only answer that would guarantee I would never have to see my mother again.

But I'll never see my Girls again either. Or Ms. Race. Or Tassie. Or Diesel or Felise.

Avery opened the door to a silver Camaro and looked back at me one more time. "Come on if you're comin'," he said. "And if you're not, don't narc on us."

He climbed into the car and slammed the door behind him. Brendan looked at me from out of the backseat and then turned away.

My legs started to shake. I'd been here before, right here where I knew I was going to go home, take a razor, and slit my wrists.

But there was no Father Dale driving up. I had to save myself this time.

I ran after the Camaro just as it pulled out from the curb. The brake lights went on, and Brendan flung open the back door.

"Get in if you're gettin'," Avery said. "You're lettin' all the cold air in."

Nobody said much on the way to Tassie's. The music was blasting pretty loud. Once I felt Brendan looking at me, but when I glanced back, he flipped his head toward the window. The loose hair above the shaved part swayed back and forth. Fletcher's did that sometimes.

My eyes started to flood, and I bit down hard on my lip. When Kenny pulled the car into Tassie's driveway, I was the first one out.

"We'll get our stuff and be right back," Avery said.

"I'll wait out here and keep the car warm," Kenny said.

Behind me, as I rushed toward the front door, I heard Brendan say, "What about gas money?"

"Don't worry about it," Kenny said. "I got bread. I always got bread."

"We're gonna be fine," Avery said. "Cheyenne, hurry up. Just take what you really need. We can buy other stuff later."

I don't have that much anyway, I thought. I was trying to force myself to go numb, not to think about what I was doing. I looked around for my backpack and realized I'd left it in the theater lobby. But I didn't need anything that was in it, and I could use a grocery bag to pack . . . what? A couple of necklaces?

I pulled out some bags from under the kitchen sink. As I passed through the living room, I could hear Avery singing in their room as if he were already auditioning for a rock band. Myself, I didn't feel like singing.

Still trying to stay stiff and unfeeling, I closed my door behind me and shook open a bag. *I don't have that much,* I kept saying to myself.

But just like a lot of other things I'd told myself—that I was a good person, that my friends were going to help me, that everything was finally going to be all right—I didn't believe that.

For openers, there was Felise's wolf mural. I'd like to have that with me wherever I went—and Felise, too.

But I made myself think about Ellie and how snotty she was to me, and I started to shove underwear into the bag.

Along with the underwear I picked up something purple. My T-shirt from Ms. Race. Holy hungers, huh?

For a minute, I couldn't stay numb. This big wave came over me; it was about the saddest I'd ever felt. I'd really been looking forward to finding out what my holy hungers were, and maybe even getting to feed some of them somehow. Anything had seemed possible that day when I was eating Ms. Race's soup . . .

Ms. Race didn't understand. That was all there was to it.

Still, I shoved the shirt in the bag.

When my clothes were packed, I'd already filled up three grocery bags. Who knew I had that much stuff? I looked around for anything else that had to go with me.

Pushing back the curtain over my cave, I felt another chest pain. I loved hiding in here, thinking and praying . . .

I'll have plenty of hiding places, I told myself. *No, I won't even have to hide!*

I poked around under there some more and came across a plate, the cookie plate Tassie had brought me that one night.

"My three favorite words are 'have a cookie,'" she had said.

I was going to miss hearing her say stuff like that.

I shook my head hard. What I wasn't going to miss was her hassling me about my mother. I had half a mind to take the cushion, even though it was really hers. I actually grabbed it and picked it up, which was when I saw my two little folded pieces of paper.

My gratitude journal. I let the cushion drop and sat down on it and picked up the pages. I tried to read them, but I couldn't see them for the blur over my eyes. Because, after all, if I was going to do this, I was going to have to leave God behind, too.

You can't tell God how you want it done, Brianna had said. *You have to do it His way.*

"But I can't do it Your way!" I whispered to the papers I was squeezing in my hands. "Don't You see that?"

I knew He didn't. Even He was not on my side. I balled up the pages and pulled back my arm to hurl them across the room. A knock on the front door stopped me in midair.

"We're comin'!" I heard Avery yell. "I'm gettin' my tapes together!"

I felt like an idiot. It was Kenny, of course. He must have gotten impatient sitting out there in his Camaro.

What does he do for a living now that he's dropped out of school to get a car like that? I thought as I crawled out of my cave and went to the door, smearing off my tears. *Maybe I can get that kind of job.*

I grunted. I didn't really want a Camaro. That wasn't one of my holy hungers. The thought went through me like a knife as I opened the door.

In front of me, Fletcher shrugged his shoulders, and said, "Hi. I was in the neighborhood and thought I'd drop by."

THERE HAD BEEN NO NEED TO SLIT MY WRISTS. I thought I was going to die right there. Actually, I thought I already had.

I couldn't run.

I couldn't throw a tantrum.

I couldn't even slam the door in his face.

I just stood there.

"Can I, like, come in?" he said. "It's really cold out here."

I saw for the first time that he wasn't wearing a coat. His lips were blue, and big red blotches were all over his face, like he had run all the way from King High.

"Sure," I said. "I was just packing."

Beyond us, as I was closing the door, a horn blew.

"I have to hurry," I said. Then I turned around and walked to my room. I must have been really close to losing it.

Fletcher followed me and stood in the bedroom doorway. He looked at the grocery bags lined up and bulging with stuff.

"Where are you going?" he said.

"I don't know," I said. I plucked fitfully at my sheets. "I'm just leaving."

"Like, you mean, running away type leaving?"

"Yeah."

Fletcher let his big, pale blue eyes roam around the room. "Why?" he said. "This is a cool place. It looks like you have it pretty good living here."

"I do," I said. "But if I don't go on my own, they're probably going to make me go back with my mother. And I can't."

"Because she abused you or something?" he said.

I leaned my head back against the bed. I was too tired all of a sudden to work at being numb. I just let the tears run down my face.

"Yeah," I said. "You don't even want to know."

"Sure I do." I waited for him to make a joke, but he didn't. He said, "If you need to talk, I mean, I want to hear it."

I was tired of telling the story. What good did it do? Except that Fletcher looked different than I'd ever seen him look before. He wasn't reaching into his pockets for something to poke me with. He wasn't grinning and calling me "amino." Matter of fact, he looked almost as miserable as I felt. I think that's why it just started coming out of me.

"She was always drunk," I said, "and she let my stepfather abuse me. Every time I'm with her it's like I turn into her, and I don't want to be like that anymore."

"Man," Fletcher said, "I'm really sorry."

He looked sorry, which got me crying hard again.

"Hey, but, man, even if you have to live with your mother," he said, "you still have your friends. Tobey and those guys, they'll still be there, you know?"

I tried to laugh, but it came out like a mushy snort. "I thought they were my friends. But they just don't get it. I guess they can't."

Fletcher shook his hair again. "What about me? I'm your amino." He tried to grin. "Why else would I cut school and come over here when I wasn't even sure this was where you went when you got in that guy's car?"

That did it. I slid down to the floor and just bawled, the way babies do when they really get going. I don't know what the poor kid would have done if somebody hadn't started pounding again, this time on my bedroom window.

"I'll tell him to hold on," Fletcher said in this tiny voice.

I kept crying, but I could hear him going to the window.

And then I heard a gasp, like Big Foot was out there or something.

Fletcher was suddenly on the floor beside me, breathing like a freight train.

"What?" I said.

"It's Brianna!" he hissed to me. "And my sister!"

"No way!" I said.

I started to lift my head, but Fletcher pushed it back down. By now, his face was as white as a bowl of pasta.

"Stay down!" he said. "Tobey can't see me cutting school, or she'll tell my dad. I'll never see the light of day till I'm twenty-one!"

"What do you want me to do?" I said.

"Don't do anything. Maybe they'll go away!"

It seemed like he was right. They stopped pounding on the window, and I started to breathe again.

Until it started on the front door. Avery stomped through the house yelling, "I'm comin', I'm comin'! Don't get your panties in a bunch!"

I was just about to get up as I heard the front door open, but the voices on the other side of it pushed me flat on the floor again.

"Hi," Tobey said, "is Cheyenne home?"

"Yeah," Avery said. "She's in her room. Tell her she had better hurry up, or we're leavin' without her."

Fletcher's eyes grew so wild I thought they were going to pop out of his head.

"I'm toast!" he whispered.

"Hide!" I said.

"Where?"

"Closet!"

I don't think he even got up off the floor. He pretty much slithered in under Ellie's blouses and pulled the door shut behind him. Not a moment too soon either. Brianna didn't even knock. Her fist was probably hurting by now.

"What are you doing, girl?" she said as she burst into my

room with Tobey behind her. "Hello" was evidently out of the question. Whats going on here!"

Tobey was looking at the three grocery bags, which were still waiting patiently inside my bedroom door. "Going somewhere?" she said.

I nodded. I was out of tears at that point.

"You really are running away, aren't you?" Brianna said.

Once again I just nodded. And, of course, I got myself ready for the lecture that was going to come out of Brianna's mouth. If I'd seen her mad at me before, that was probably nothing compared to what she was about to be now.

But she didn't yell. She didn't even look like she wanted to smack me up the side of the head. She just closed her eyes and pressed her lips together. For a stunned second, I thought *she* was going to cry.

"I came down too hard on you," she said. "I gave you the idea, didn't I?"

"No," I said. "Avery did."

Tobey jabbed a thumb toward the door. "That precious little child with the attitude?"

"Yeah. Look . . ." I tried to swallow. "I know you're going to tell me it's stupid, and maybe it is to you. But you just don't know. I can't face even thinking about living with my mother again. You don't know what it was like—"

"Can we sit down or something?" Brianna said. "You don't have a plane to catch, do you?"

For the first time, I actually smiled. "Not hardly," I said. "Kenny drives like he's flying a plane, but—"

"Okay," Tobey cut in. "Come on, grab that cushion and sit down."

I sat on my precious pillow and clung to its sides. Tobey and Brianna parked on the floor facing me.

"You ran off today before I could finish," Brianna said. "See, I wasn't sayin' we wouldn't help you. I just wanted you to look at some other options."

"I don't have any other options," I said.

She clenched her hands. She was trying really hard to be patient. "You don't know that," she said. "What if your mother has really changed? Did she sound like her old self in her letters?"

I couldn't answer. I wasn't sure. I'd tried to keep the letters as just words—not sounds that I wouldn't be able to push out of my head.

"I also think you've gotten ahead of yourself," Tobey said. "Nobody's telling you that you have to live with her. She's asking for an hour."

"But it's a waste of time," I said. "If I don't ever want to be with her again, period, why even try?"

They looked at each other, like they had been discussing that very question between them. "We just feel like God is saying you need to give her a chance," Brianna said.

"No," I said. "Maybe you guys could do that because you're these good people, but I—"

"You are a good person, an incredible person!" Tobey said. She shook back her hair, like she was getting down to serious business. "You're so generous you'd risk getting in trouble to get something for somebody. That lady in the bead shop saw what kind of person you were even before you went in there and confessed that you had ripped her off. She said she took to you from the beginning."

"Which brings me to another thought that you can't ignore, girl," Brianna said. Her eyes were bright, the way really wise people's get when they're about to say something that's going to blow you away. I gripped the sides of the cushion so that whatever she said wouldn't change my mind.

"This just came to me—and I think it's what's been bothering me the whole time," Brianna said. "That woman—what was her name?"

"Elena."

"That Elena, she forgave you for stealing from her, and you just lit up like you had fireworks in your face. You were ready to go for it after that."

"I would have, too—and I still want to," I said. "But I can't do it with—

"Oh, would you hush up for just one minute, girl?" Brianna put her hands on my knees. "The point is how do you expect God to keep forgiving you, if even when other people forgive you for stuff, you won't try to forgive your own mother?"

"She said 'try,'" Tobey pointed out. "Not 'go back and live with her' or 'be her best friend.' Just see what your mom has to say."

A thud came from the direction of the closet. Brianna and Tobey glanced around and then focused back on me. But my heart dropped.

Fletcher had just heard that whole thing. It was bad enough I had told him my mother was an alcoholic. Now he knew I was a thief. Great.

"Hey, girl, pay attention," Brianna said. Her voice was getting crisp again. She was sitting up tall and talking with her hands. I knew better than to do anything but listen.

"Now," she said, "are you ever going to steal again?"

"No!" I said. I hoped Fletcher heard that loud and clear.

"Why not?"

"Because," I said, "even if I thought about it, I'd see that lady's face. She was like this angel."

"And what if she hadn't forgiven you?" Brianna said. "You might do it again, right? You might be ticked off enough or figure what's the use in even trying to be a decent person."

My eyes went from one of them to the other. They weren't taking their own eyes off me. I either had to answer honestly or I was really done. And even running away couldn't erase that.

"I might," I said. "Yeah. Okay, I probably would. But what if I just can't forgive her? What if I see her, and it's the same old thing?"

Brianna grabbed for my hands. Tobey was immediately by my side with her arm around me.

"Maybe you won't be able to. Maybe you'll just have to give it to God," Brianna said. "But you definitely never will if you don't at least see her. Besides—" She sat up and smiled, really big. "You don't think we're going to make you go it alone, do you?"

I stared at her. "That's what it sounded like at lunch."

Tobey and Brianna looked at each other solemnly. "I am so sorry about that, Cheyenne," Tobey said. "We really messed up, and we just sat there after you left feeling like trash. But I think we're back on track now." She stood up and snatched one of the grocery bags. "We'll prove it; we'll help you unpack."

Before I could open my mouth to stop her, she was at the closet and throwing open the door to reveal Fletcher standing there, arms hugged around himself. He lifted a hand, waved, and said, "Hi, Sis."

"What the—!" Tobey cried.

Just then a horn blew out front again, and everybody's attention turned to the door.

For me, it was now or never.

I bolted from the floor and flew to the living room. The front door was still standing open, and I leaned out.

Avery was in the Camaro with his whole upper body sticking out the window. "Are you comin' or not?" he said. "We gotta get out of here before Tassie comes home!"

Behind me, nobody said anything. I could feel them standing there, waiting for me to make a decision. Run or face the worst ordeal I could dream of.

With them always behind me.

I hugged the doorframe and shook my head at Avery. He shook his back. The words "You're a psycho" were clearly etched on his face.

As I closed the door and heard the Camaro screech off down the street, I thought how I wasn't going to miss that kid at all. Brendan, now, that might be another story. He might be okay without Avery dragging him down.

Without the kind of friends I had, I could have been just like Brendan.

I turned around and threw myself at Brianna. She folded her arms around me, and we danced around the living room squealing. I could vaguely hear Tobey saying, "You have some explaining to do, pal."

"And you don't?" Fletcher said. "Where's *your* off-campus pass?"

Brianna stopped swinging me around and looked at her watch. "We better get back. We'll figure out the explaining part later."

We piled into Lazarus, and Tobey handed me the Kleenex box. I was blowing my nose as we pulled out of the driveway.

Then Brianna said, "Who's that dude?"

She was pointing toward our front door. It was Brendan, running down the steps and waving at us. Tobey stopped the car, and I rolled down my window.

"What are you doing here?" I said. "I thought you went with Avery!"

"I didn't."

"No kidding," Fletcher mumbled.

"How come?" I said.

"Uh, could you guys discuss this a little later?" Tobey said. "We have to get back, and you're freezing the whole car. My heater barely works as it is."

"Can I have a ride back to school?" Brendan said.

"Sure," Tobey said.

I slid over—so that I was pressed next to Fletcher, I might add—and Brendan clambered in. He didn't say anything all the way to King, but I could tell from the relieved way he sighed he felt just the way I did: like we'd both barely missed making a really, really big mistake.

I whispered, "Thank You, God."

BRENDAN DISAPPEARED AS SOON AS WE GOT INSIDE the front door of the school. The rest of us went straight to Ms. Race's desk. The minute she saw us, she pulled me into her arms and held me. If I hadn't already been worn out from crying, I would have been boo-hooing all over the place. Besides, I felt hopeful now.

The other secretaries were giving weird looks; so Ms. Race pushed us into Mr. Holden's office and shut the door.

"We only cut one class," Fletcher said. "How come we have to see the principal?"

"He's gone for the day," Ms. Race said. "Now tell me what's going on."

We did, with all of us talking at once. The closer we got to the end, the darker Ms. Race's face grew and the tighter my chest. I'd never seen her look so annoyed at us before.

"What am I going to do with you guys?" she said when we were done. She sat back in her chair and pushed up the sleeves of her sweater. "Anything could have happened. The truant officers could have nabbed all four of you. Tassie could have come home, and you would have put her in a terrible position. And you—" She zeroed in on me. I could feel myself shrinking. "Running away? You haven't heard what happens to young girls who go to the streets?"

"Yeah," I said lamely. "I wasn't thinking about that."

"But none of that happened, Ms. Race," Brianna said. "I

know it was stupid, but it just didn't seem like we had any other choice."

"Yeah!" Fletcher said.

Tobey glared at him, and he shut up.

Ms. Race pressed her fingers to her temples. "I know. I'm just venting. We mothers have to do that, you know."

"You're a great mom," Tobey said.

"Well, that doesn't mean you're off the hook, any of you."

Ms. Race took us in with her serious eyes. We all shook our heads.

"All right. After school I want you all to report right back here for detention," she said. "It's almost the end of fifth period. I'll write you passes to get back in, but you're going to have to bring in notes from your parents tomorrow."

Fletcher groaned. "I'm dead."

"I doubt that," Ms. Race said. "Remember, be back here at two-fifteen and not a minute later."

"I thought they had detention in the study hall," Brianna said.

"Not this detention," Ms. Race said.

Her face was still so solemn I wasn't about to question anything. She could have said we were going to have to scrub the cafeteria floor with our tongues, and I wouldn't have said a word.

The bell rang just as I walked into my math class. Mr. Hopkins took the hall pass, stuck it in his drawer, and pointed to the board. "There's your homework," he said.

Just like that. The rest of the world was going on as if I hadn't almost trashed my life. I could do my homework tonight. I could eat Tassie's tuna casserole. I could sleep in my own bed.

I was going to be up half the night writing all *that* stuff on the list.

When my last class was finally over, I hurried back to Ms. Race's office. She handed me my backpack, which she had picked up in the theater lobby after I'd run out, but she didn't say anything else as she went into the conference room.

"She's really pensive," Tobey whispered behind me.

"What's 'pensive'?" I said.

"Uptight," Norie said. "I could feel it the minute I walked in here."

I jumped about a foot. "What are you doing here?" I said. "How come you have detention? Don't tell me you were out looking for me someplace. Dude, I feel like such a loser getting everybody into trouble . . ."

"Cheyenne, zip," Norie said. "I'm not here for detention. We're having a Flagpole meeting."

Even as she said it, Shannon and Marissa hurried into the office, and Wyatt joined Norie. Then Ira showed up and Diesel. I tried to duck, but he would have pulled me out of the bottom of a well if he had had to. His forehead was so far down over his eyes you could barely see them, but I knew they were mad.

"What did you think you were doin'?" he said. "Why didn't you come find me instead of running off with Avery? You know he's trouble. What, do you walk around that house with your ears plugged up?"

"Wow, Diesel," Tobey said. "That's the most I've ever heard you say."

"I got a lot more to say," he growled.

I myself was adding this to my gratitude list. I sure loved it when Diesel said he loved me.

Ms. Race shooed us all into the conference room. Everybody got really quiet, I guess because it seemed strange for Ms. Race to look so—what was that word—"pensive."

Tobey obviously couldn't stand it. As soon as Fletcher and Brianna got there and Ms. Race closed the door, Tobey said, "We are so sorry we upset you, Ms. Race. I know we weren't thinking. We were just trying to keep Cheyenne from getting hurt."

Ms. Race sank into one of the padded chairs and rolled

herself up to the table. For the first time, I saw her eyes were shiny with tears she hadn't let fall.

"I know; I know all that," she said. "I should just thank God you're all safe, but it's so hard, knowing how close you came—especially you, Cheyenne. I just shudder to think about what could have happened."

"Now I'm surprised at you, Ms. Race," Brianna said.

Ms. Race was the one who looked surprised. "Why?" she said.

"Because. Far as I see it, God took care of Cheyenne this afternoon. I don't go around cuttin' class—and you *know* Tobey doesn't. I just felt like God was saying, 'Do what you have to do, Brianna.' "

"Can I say something?"

We all looked at Marissa.

"Okay, God took care of you guys and all that, but . . ." She looked down at her hands, folded on the table. "I think we also have to take responsibility. We can't just say, 'God's going to take care of us' and then go off without thinking."

It seemed like I should say something. I didn't know how I was going to with the pain in my chest, but I raised my hand.

"What are you doing?" Norie said. "Just talk. You're still part of this group."

"I wasn't thinking God would take care of me," I said. "I was thinking I had to leave Him behind because I knew what I was doing wasn't okay with Him. I just didn't see any other way—but I think I was wrong."

"No foolin'!" Brianna was looking absolutely purple. Ira put his hand on her arm so she wouldn't fly across the table at me.

"Cheyenne," Ms. Race said. She had her eyes closed while she was talking. "I cannot tell you how glad I am to hear you say that. And darlin', I forgive you. I really do."

Dude, we all started bawling then. Except for Fletcher and Ira. They both just looked kind of nauseous. Diesel, though, blew his nose once or twice, and Wyatt just went ahead and let some tears go. Brianna held up her hand before we got carried away.

"All right. What I want to know is what we're going to do now." She directed her eyes at me. "And you notice I said 'we,' girl. All of us are going to help you through this. But you have to promise that you're not going to flip out and run off when the going gets tough."

"And you have to talk to us," Tobey said.

"And definitely no more 'I can't,' " Norie said. "You can say 'I'm scared,' or 'it's hard,' but no 'I can't.' I hate that."

"Do you think God hates it?" Shannon said.

"Definitely."

"Wow."

"Back to the subject," Tobey said. "We have a Plan of Action to do. Who has some paper?"

"I do," Ms. Race said. She produced a roll of white paper and a Tupperware thing full of markers. Marissa chose a couple and got ready to write.

"Heads," Norie said.

We bowed them, holding hands, and we prayed.

Then a Plan of Action unfolded that made me feel like maybe, just maybe, I could do this after all.

And if I couldn't, plenty of people were there to pick me up.

It was getting dark out when the janitor poked his head in the conference room and asked us how much longer we were going to be because he had to vacuum in there. Tobey rolled up the Plan and promised to bring it over tonight. Diesel told me I was riding with him, and everybody swarmed around me and gave me hugs. Over Wyatt's shoulder I saw Fletcher.

He was bolting out the door without even looking behind him.

I thought sadly, *Now that he knows about the shoplifting and all, he doesn't want to have anything to do with me. I was right all along.*

I let out a long sigh that made Shannon squeeze me harder. I guess she thought I was sobbing. I was just letting go. I could almost hear Elena saying, "One good thing—my friends—is better than another thing that will never be."

"You're going to do everything we decided, right?" Diesel said to me on the way home.

"Right," I said. "I'd be stupid not to, and you know what, Diesel?"

He grunted.

"I'm tired of being stupid."

"That's a trip," he said. "I never thought you were stupid to begin with."

When we reached the house, Diesel did his part. He shoved Ellie, Felise, and Brendan in the truck and went down to Round Table to get pizza. Tassie growled about all the trouble she had gone to make potato soup, until she found out why she and I had to be alone.

I sat down at the kitchen table with her, and I told her all about my stealing from the bead shop. I didn't skip a detail because that had been my promise to the group, to God, and to myself. No matter what Tassie had to do once I told her, I had to say it all. And you know what she did?

She nodded her white head until her bobbed hair swayed, and she said, "Where is this angel woman? I want to take her some cookies."

I stared. "That's it? You aren't going to ground me or send me back to Wittenberg or something?"

"Why would I want to do that?" she said. "You've already punished yourself worse than I'd even think of. All that abuse you had growin' up, Cheyenne, you've turned it on yourself." She reached for a pad and a pencil. "I have to call foster care tomorrow. Until you're old enough to get a job, you have to have an allowance. Girl your age has to have some spendin' money."

I was shaking my head. "I don't think I ought to be re-warded, Tassie."

She drilled her very blue eyes into me. "You just keep saying thank You to the Lord," she said. "And don't throw things back at Him when He gives them to you."

"Oh," I said. I could feel a smile spreading across my face. It felt so good to smile again.

We were barely done talking when Tobey and Brianna arrived. Both of them were looking at me with all these questions in their eyes, but my grin answered them.

"Tassie says you guys can help," I said.

"I'm grateful for you two," Tassie said to them. "I got this other mess to deal with now. When that boy comes home, he's going to think detention was a trip to Disneyland." Then she went to look for the number of the halfway house for me.

Tobey squeezed my hand. "Are you scared?"

"Yeah," I said.

"I'm glad you said that, or I'd have known you were lying," Brianna said. "My heart's pounding, and it isn't even my mama!"

"Just remember, we're right here praying," Tobey said.

Like I was going to forget that now. Tassie handed me the phone and the number, and they all went into the living room to sit on the love seats. I dialed and then reminded myself to breathe. I was surprised I could.

"Robinson House," somebody said on the other end of the line.

"Uh, hi," I said. "This is Cheyenne. Cheyenne Jackson. Um, could I please speak to Valerie Jackson, if she can come to the phone or whatever."

"Of course!"

The voice sounded cheerful, as if I were calling my mother at a neighbor's or something. They had never been that cheerful at Wittenberg, or even at the group home in Yerington. I'd kind of halfway hoped they wouldn't let me talk to her.

You just have to do this, Cheyenne, I told myself. *And you have to do it now.*

"Hello?" said a voice.

I frowned. "I need to speak to Valerie Jackson. I think she lives there."

"This is Valerie Jackson." There was a pause, like she was catching her breath. "Is that you, Cheyenne?"

"Yes," I said. "It's me. I didn't, like, recognize your voice."

"I didn't recognize yours either! You sound so . . . grown up."

"I'm fourteen," I said.

That was stupid. She was my mother. I should hope to shout she would know how old I was. Although, after you had poured that much liquor into your brain, you might not . . .

Stop it! I told myself. *You're supposed to give her a chance.*

"Are you still there?" she said.

"Yes," I said. "Sorry. I was just . . . Anyway, I got your letter."

"Good. I wasn't sure since I hadn't heard back from you. Which is all right . . . I mean, I understand—"

"You're hearing back from me now," I said. "I thought I'd call you instead."

"Oh, I'm so glad you did. It's good to hear your voice. I can hear you in there now that you're talking some more."

I sure couldn't hear *her*. This woman still sounded nothing like my mother. Her voice was kind of pulled back, sort of quavery the way Norie's got like once in a century when she was freaked out about something. I decided they must have her on some kind of medication there at the Robinson House.

"Well anyway," I said. "You wanted to see me—I mean, you wanted us to get together?"

"I would love that." She did that catching-her-breath thing again. "I'm not trying to push, you know. I just thought it would be . . . nice."

"Okay," I said.

I sure wished Tobey and Brianna were standing next to me with cue cards. I turned around and looked into the living room. They were both there with Tassie, and all three of them had their heads bowed. Dude.

"So, what about this Saturday?" I said.

"All right. If that's convenient for you."

"Sure. Can you get to the Denny's on Wells?"

"I can get anywhere you want."

"That's a good place then." Actually, Ira had said it would be a good place. He said kids from King never went there. So I wouldn't have gawkers.

"Two o'clock?" I said.

"Fine." That was the first time she sounded a little disappointed. Wyatt had said what about having lunch with her, but I wasn't sure I wanted it to go on that long, not this time. It was like my mother knew that. Go figure.

"Then I guess I'll see you Saturday," I said.

"I am so looking forward to it," she said. "This will get me through the week."

"Oh," I said. "Well, that's good." I was feeling more lame by the second, and it was time to hang up. Obviously, I was going to have to be the one to end the call because she sounded as if she wanted to hang on for days.

"Well, 'bye," I said.

" 'Bye, Cheyenne," she said. "I'll see you Saturday."

Tobey and Brianna were in the kitchen before I could even hang up the phone.

"That didn't sound too bad," Tobey said. "I mean, we weren't exactly listening but—"

"You didn't stand up and tell her where to go," Brianna said. "That's a good sign."

"You all right?" Tassie said.

She brushed her hand across my shoulder, and I reached up and grabbed it and clung to it. "I don't know," I said. "It was like I was talking to some stranger, you know?"

"You kind of were," Tobey said. "I mean, if she was always drunk, you never knew the real her."

I nodded, but even as I did, a vision of a little girl sitting on the ground, picking up pieces of cloth for a smiling, long-haired woman with paint under her nails to make into a doll flickered across my screen. Just as quickly it faded out, and I looked up at Tassie. "Did Avery come home yet?"

She shook her head and pressed her lips together. I looked at Brianna and Tobey. They were both giving me now-is-the-time nods.

"I don't think he's going to come back unless you go after him," I said. "I didn't tell you this at first because I thought he'd give it up and come home—"

"What are you sayin', Cheyenne?" Tassie said.

"He said he was running away," I said. "Some guy named Kenny told him he would take him to Sacramento."

"How do you know all this?" she said. "Does Brendan know?"

I nodded. "Yeah. We both almost went with him."

Tassie took my head in her hands and cradled it against her enormous chest. "Thank the Lord some of you kids have some sense," she said. "Thank the Lord above."

Then she let go and went for the phone. "Would you girls excuse me?" she said.

That night, when we all went to bed, Ellie obviously had insomnia over the Avery thing. "Did he really run away?" she whispered to me in the dark.

I looked up from my flashlight and my gratitude list. "I guess so. I thought he would chicken out."

"He's too dumb to be scared," Felise said.

"Boy, you got that right," Ellie said. "Tassie's, like, medieval about a lot of things, but we don't have it that bad."

"No," I said to my already-filled-up page. "We sure don't."

This time I said it aloud: "Thank You, God."

"You are so weird," Ellie said.

But she fell asleep.

Every day that week the Flagpole Girls—and Guys— prayed at lunch. And somebody went home with me every day to work on the Plan. We were trying to feed my holy hungers.

Number one: I wanted my mother to know I had grown up a lot, and that I wouldn't be content to live a shabby life with no self-respect anymore. Shannon offered to let me borrow some of her clothes, but I didn't think that would be honest. So she helped me pull together an outfit from my own stuff.

"You don't think I'd look stupid with this T-shirt under overalls?" I said.

"You look incredible in purple," Shannon said. "What necklace do you have? Oh, and what about sewing some beads on a jeans jacket?"

"I don't have a jeans jacket."

"You do now." She grinned and pulled one out of her backpack. It had a familiar smell to it.

"Where did you get that?" I said, wrinkling my nose.

"Diesel said to give it to you. It doesn't fit him anymore. We'll have to wash it, of course."

"About eight times," I said. But I was grinning. This was going to be so perfect.

And in some pretty amazing ways. That night I was taking apart an old necklace to use the beads for my jacket when Ellie came in and asked me what I was doing. When I told her, she shook her head at me.

"I know," I said. "You think I'm weird."

"I do," she said. She rolled her way-made-up eyes. "But I was just thinking if you really want to show your mother you're getting your act together, you ought to let me help you with your hair."

I pulled out a straggly end and looked at it. "Good luck," I said.

"I hate to have to say this, but you have a great face. You just hide it all the time. Here."

She stuck me in front of her mirror under her bed and

went after my hair with a brush. I have to admit, it was pretty awesome, watching my face come out from under my bangs. She swept it back up into a scrunchie and took a curling iron to my ends. I had to smile at myself.

"You disgust me," she said. "You look like a model or something. I really hate you."

She smiled—now that's something you don't see that often—and dug around in her makeup bag. "You don't need that much makeup, but you ought to play up your lips. I'd kill for those lips. In fact, watch yourself while you're sleeping."

"Gross!" I said, covering my mouth.

"Don't be a geek. Put your hand down, and I'll stick some gloss on there. Ooh, nice."

It *was* nice. I wanted to hug her. But I didn't push my luck.

Holy hunger number two: I wanted my mother to know I never wanted to go hungry again or have to worry about where the next meal was coming from. On the day Marissa came, we got busy in the kitchen and came out with a pile of cookies to take to Valerie.

It really seemed to calm Tassie down. She had called everybody but the governor of California, but there was still no sign of Avery.

I said to her, "I bet if I'd told you sooner, you might have found him."

But she wouldn't hear it. "You aren't responsible for that boy's foolishness. I'm just thankful you and Brendan are still here."

Brendan actually looked a little thankful himself. I heard different music coming out of his room now, and he said more than two words at the dinner table without Avery there to talk for him. Diesel even started to drive him to school.

"What do I have to do to rate that?" Ellie said.

"Get a personality transplant," Diesel said. Then he grinned at her and told her to get in the truck—but just this once.

Holy hunger number three: I wanted my mother to know

I didn't want to be around abusive men anymore. I wanted to feel safe.

On Norie's day, she brought Wyatt, Brianna, and Ira with her. We had this big long talk in the living room about the way it was going to go down on Saturday.

"Ira and I are going to escort you into Denny's," Wyatt said. "My mother always said if I didn't turn out to be a gentleman she was going to put me up for adoption; so I learned this stuff."

"He did," Norie said. "Here I am, this feminist, and he's holding doors open for me and pulling out chairs."

"I can dig that," Ira said.

"You don't do it for me," Brianna said.

"You want me to?"

She got this coy look on her face. "Sometimes . . . maybe."

The whole thing was making me kind of sad, in a way. Here they were, these happy couples with these healthy relationships. I'd never thought that would ever happen for me so I hadn't thought about it that much. But now that I'd had those few minutes here and there with Fletcher treating me like I was this *girl*, I kind of had a longing for it—with him.

But Fletcher hadn't been in sight since the day of the Plan of Action meeting. All that talk about being my amino seemed to have gone down the toilet once he heard about my "record."

I sighed. Oh well. I could look at him in Spanish class. Wow.

"Cheyenne, are you listening, girl?" Brianna said.

"No," I said. "What are we talking about?"

"We're talking about how Wyatt and Ira are going to hold doors open for you and pull out chairs for you and treat you like this little queen when you go meet your mother," Norie said. She squinted. "Is that too cheesy?"

"No," I said. "I don't care what it does for my mother; it sounds good to me."

Holy hunger number four was really the most important,

and by Saturday noon, even after I was dressed in my clean, beaded jacket and Ellie had done my hair and my lip gloss, I hadn't figured out how I was going to get it across.

I wanted my mother to know I'd found God and I wanted to live a God-filled life. Wouldn't you know, Ms. Race was the one who came up with the answer.

She arrived about one o'clock with a gift bag in her hand. "I brought you something."

"You already gave me the shirt," I said.

"Well, you just keep saying thank you and all kinds of things come your way." She crinkled her eyes at me.

I dug into the bag and pulled out a notebook that was covered in some kind of coarse cloth with all these bright colors on it.

"Did you get this in South America?" I said.

"I bought the fabric in Guatemala," she said. "I've been waiting a year to find out why I bought it, and last night I knew. Open it up."

I did, but only blank pieces of binder paper were inside. I wasn't as slow by then as I used to be. I grinned up at her. "Gratitude journal," I said.

"Right. I thought you could put the pages you've already done right in there."

I raced to my bedroom like a little kid and snatched up my pages from under the cushion. The two crinkled ones were pretty smoothed out by now. I took them into the living room and snapped them into the journal. The whole routine seemed to give me an idea.

"You know what?" I said.

"No," Ms. Race said, eyes shining. "But I bet you're about to tell me."

"I could take this with me. If my mother asks me what it is, I could tell her and that way she'll know that I'm a God-person now."

"I love it," she said. "Now, I have something else for you, but this isn't a gift. It's an advance payment."

She pulled a ten-dollar bill out of her pocket. "I want you to make me some earrings. We can go to the bead store together and pick out the materials; this is just for labor. I thought you might want it now in case you decide to treat your mother to a soda or something." Ms. Race folded it into my lifeless hand. "It will make her happy to know you're so ambitious."

I promised myself I'd start daydreaming about what I'd put together as soon as I got back.

Tobey arrived next, and she went over the prayer we had let God give us, the one I was going to say to myself over and over when I was walking toward my mother: *Lord, help me to forgive like You do.*

By 1:30, everyone was there, trying to be calm and make me laugh. I laughed plenty. I giggled, actually, but that should be no surprise. Still, my chest felt like somebody was standing on it. I was so scared.

Brianna took both my hands and squeezed them. "Keep talking, girl," she said. "Don't let it get to you."

"You promise she's not going to make me go off with her?" I said. "This one visit doesn't mean I'm saying I want to be with her?"

"That's right," she said. "And if she tries to do something illegal, you know the guys will be right there."

"I'd be there, too," Tassie said, "but I'm like a hostage here, waitin' for word on Avery."

"That's okay," I said. "He's in more trouble than I am."

"We can pray for him, too," Tobey said. "As long as we're all going to be here."

My pray-ers nodded: Shannon, Marissa, Tobey, Brianna, Norie, Ms. Race, and Tassie. They all went into a blur in front of me.

"How can this get messed up?" I said. "I mean, it can't with all this praying going on!"

"Heavy," Diesel said.

I think that was kind of like "Amen."

"I think we should pray now, before you guys go," Tobey said.

"Absolutely," Norie said. "Come on. Hands. Heads."

I giggled and slipped my sweaty hands into Tobey's and Brianna's. Norie was already leading off when somebody pounded on the door.

"Dear Lord, let it be about Avery," Tassie said.

We held our breath like we all had one set of lungs as Tassie went to the door. When she opened it, though, it wasn't Avery.

It was Fletcher.

"IT'S ABOUT TIME," TOBEY SAID. "IS DAD COMING IN?"

"He has a meeting," Fletcher said. "But he said to tell you he was praying for you."

For the first time in exactly four days and twenty-one hours, Fletcher looked at me.

I whispered, "Thank you."

Tobey was whispering, too, and so was Norie.

"Did you bring it? Where is it?" Tobey asked Fletcher.

In fact, everybody seemed to know what was happening except me.

"What's going on?" I said.

They all looked at Fletcher, who gulped so hard I could see his Adam's apple go up and down. "I brought you something," he said. He looked about two years younger than usual with all these people staring at him. And more adorable than ever.

"You did?" I said.

"You didn't know?" Norie said. She punched Fletcher lightly on the shoulder. "Way to go, Fletch. You actually kept a secret."

"We were sure he would blab," Marissa said. She gave her nervous little laugh.

"How was I going to blab?" he said. "You told me if I talked to her at all I'd tell for sure. Why do you think I haven't spoken to her all week?"

"*What?*" Tobey said. She gave him the most disgusted, big-sister look I'd seen her give him yet. "You are so lame! Just what she needed!"

"Did you think he was mad at you, Cheyenne?" Shannon said.

You don't even know the half of it, I wanted to say. But I just giggled. Not only was Fletcher L'Orange adorable, funny, and sensitive—but he was as much of a dipstick as I was. We were going to get along just fine.

"Give it to her, Fletch," Wyatt said. "We have to get going."

Fletcher dug into his pocket and pulled out his fist, which he held out to me.

I opened my hands, no questions asked. If he put a scorpion in them, he would get mobbed, so I figured I could trust him.

It wasn't a scorpion anyway. It was a string of beads with some pewter letters between them. I spread them out on my palm, and my face spread open in a smile. It was a bracelet, made up of turquoise beads, each one separated by a letter. "*Amigo,*" it spelled.

"Just so you don't forget," Fletcher said. "I don't know; it might help."

" 'Might'?" I said. "No, it definitely will."

Then I couldn't help it. I threw my arms around his neck. Even with all those people standing around going "Ah!" he put his arms around me, too. I don't know how long we would have hugged if Wyatt hadn't said, "I hate to break this up but . . ."

We scrambled back into our circle. Tassie was in it with us, but I noticed that Felise, Ellie, and Brendan were in the room, too, kind of shuffling around in the background.

"Come on in, you guys," I said to them. "You don't have to say anything. It's cool." I guess it would have been way too awkward not to, so they slid in with their heads down and took people's hands like they were being offered Brussels sprouts. Still, it felt good to have my whole family in there. All my holy hungers were being filled.

When we were done, I got one more round of hugs. Ellie and Brendan made it a point to be out in the kitchen when that happened. Felise, though, stood there. Mind you, she looked like she was waiting to go into the dentist's office, but she actually put her arms out to me. When I went to her, she said to me, "I didn't do nothin' for ya. I just wanted to say good luck."

"You're my sister," I said. "You do stuff for me all the time."

"She's weird," Ellie whispered as she swept by.

Felise and I looked at each other, and we laughed. It was a cool moment.

Wyatt finally got me out the door, and we piled into Tassie's big old van.

"Why don't we just take your truck?" I said as I strapped myself into the front seat.

"There isn't room," Diesel said.

I craned my neck around, about ready to point out that he couldn't count. But three people were in the back: Ira, Wyatt, and Fletcher.

"Do you care if I come?" Fletcher said. He reached for his already fastened seat belt, but Wyatt waxed him lightly across the head.

"Just stay where you are, Tex," Wyatt said. "Don't blow it."

I grinned to myself, and then I have to say that was the last thought I gave to Fletcher for a while. I started to whisper my prayer to myself: *Lord, help me to forgive her like You do.*

The trip to Denny's was way too short. It was like God had cleared away all the traffic on I-80 or something. We pulled into a parking place, and Diesel turned off the engine, but nobody moved. They were all looking at me like they thought I was going to back out.

"All right," I said. "Let's go."

Don't let my this-is-no-big-deal attitude fool you. On the

188   Nancy Rue

inside, I was barely holding myself together. In fact, if it had been just up to me, I never would have walked through the door. But with all those people back at Tassie's praying and the four gorgeous dudes sitting in the truck with me, I made it.

Wyatt held open the door, and he and Ira went inside with me. Diesel said he would wait in the van, just in case I wanted to get out of there fast. Fletcher looked at them all for instructions.

"Why don't you stick with me?" Diesel said. "I can tell you a thing or two about women."

"Cool," Fletcher said.

Denny's was warm inside, but my legs were still shaking. I straightened them real tight and looked around.

"You see her anywhere?" Wyatt whispered to me. His hand was gently touching my elbow, which was reassuring.

I shook my head. "There's nobody here that looks like my mother."

"What about her?" Ira said.

I looked where he was nodding. A woman who had been sitting on the bench where people wait for a table stood up. But it wasn't her; it wasn't Valerie. This woman was tiny, and she had short, dark hair with gray streaks in it. She was too old, too small, too frail. And too frightened looking.

"She's coming over here," Wyatt whispered. "You sure that's not her?"

I looked for baggy eyes. There were none. I checked for a puffy face. Nothing. I searched for a glazed look, a hint of simmering anger, or a shadow of a black life hanging over her. I didn't see any of that. I only saw blue paint under the woman's fingernails.

It was my mother.

"Cheyenne," she said. Her voice sounded just like I felt inside: ready to shake right off into nothing. But I didn't even think about running. I took a step forward and said, "Hi. I'm here."

"You are," she said.

She stood there staring at me, though not with that blind expression I'd gotten used to. She looked more like she had never seen me before, or anyone like me. She must have caught herself, or else I was looking back with a what-are-you-looking-at expression on my face because she suddenly turned all blotchy-skinned and said, "I'm sorry. I'm being rude. Are these your friends?"

I nodded. "Yeah, this is Ira, and this is Wyatt. They brought me over."

Wyatt reached out and shook her hand, and so did Ira. She looked impressed.

"You all right, Cheyenne?" Wyatt said.

I was pretty sure I was. We had been standing there facing each other for a whole minute, and I hadn't started to bite my nails yet. I nodded at him.

"We'll just hang out at the counter," Ira said. "Come on, Wyatt, I'll buy you a Coke."

They moved away, and the waitress gave us a questioning look. "You two want a table?" she said.

"I guess so, sure," I said.

"Smoking or non?"

"Non," I said firmly.

My mother followed me to the table the waitress took us to and sat down across from me, but she didn't put the napkin in her lap or even glance at the menu the girl left. She just sat there looking kind of terrified.

I've thought about skipping over this next part and not including it in my story, but that wouldn't be honest. It wouldn't tell the whole story if I left it out.

You see, right then, when she was rubbing her hands together and trying to smile and then not smile, I knew she was scared. The bad part is, for a mean, little minute, I was glad.

How many times had she let me be scared so bad I thought I was going to die? How many times had she stood in my bedroom doorway in Winnemucca and listened to me scream while Julius hit me?

For a minute, it seemed only fair.

But only for a minute. I guess God got in there. I know she did—Valerie. She put her hands up to her face and breathed hard. It was that thing she had done on the phone.

"Uh, are you okay?" I said.

After a second she nodded and took down her hands. Her eyes were watery.

"I promised myself I wasn't going to do that," she said. "I guess the promises you make to yourself are the hardest ones to keep."

Now that surprised me. "Yeah," I said. "I guess."

It did occur to me to add, *Although you never were too good at keeping the ones you made to me either.* But I didn't. I couldn't. Maybe it was because I still wasn't convinced this was the same woman they had taken me away from. This was just a sad person who looked as if she had lost everything. I mean it, that was the way she looked. She didn't even know where to put her hands, she was so lost. First they were up on the table, then in her lap, then massaging the menu that she didn't open. A thought sizzled through my mind: *She has nothing, and I have everything. How sad.*

I cleared my throat and said, "So, how are you?"

She burst into tears. I mean burst. Ira and Wyatt turned around from the counter, but I nodded to them I was okay. It was my mother who wasn't.

"Are you all right?" I said. "Are you supposed to, like, take a pill or something?"

"No, no, no, I'm fine." She snatched up the napkin and dabbed her eyes, although they just kept streaming. "I am perfect, in fact, because I am sitting across from my daughter—and even if she hates me now, it's enough just to be sitting here and having her ask me how I am."

Dude. She knew. I'd never ever said it to her, but she knew

I'd hated her. At least she understood one thing about me—about the way I used to feel.

But I didn't feel like that now. This poor thing wasn't somebody you hated. This was somebody you felt sorry for. And I did, big-time.

"I don't hate you," I said. "I used to, but not now. I mean it, I don't."

Valerie shook her head. "Maybe not, but I don't see how you can ever forgive me. *Darn* it! I wasn't going to get into all this today. I just wanted us to have a nice conversation!"

"No way!" I said. It suddenly felt as if I was going to have to be in charge. Go figure. "No way," I said again. "How are we supposed to have a 'nice conversation' when there's this big wall between us? We have to talk about this stuff or else it just builds up, and then you explode. At least I do—I don't know about you—I don't know anything about you anymore. But if I don't talk stuff out, forget it. I get nasty, I get stupid, I make bad decisions. It gets ugly."

She was smiling through her tears. A glimmer of something from way back on the desert was on her lips. It was weird, too, that at that moment I noticed we had the same lips. The ones everybody was always raving about.

"I am so glad to see you haven't changed in one respect, Cheyenne," she said. "You can still talk the ears off a donkey. And I love it. Did I ever tell you I loved that about you?"

"No," I said. "Not that I can remember."

It got sullen between us again. She looked as if she were groping for a life preserver. "I know I destroyed your childhood. I don't expect you to forgive me. That isn't even why I wanted to see you. I just wanted to look at you, you know?"

I waited for my chest to tighten up, or for a rude answer to run through my mind. Nothing happened, except that the word *forgive* got stuck in a little crevice in my brain, and all the things I'd heard about forgiveness seemed to be calling out from it.

What if Angel Lady hadn't forgiven you? What then?
You are clean because God cleanses you.

How can you expect God to keep on forgiving you if you can't even try to forgive your own mother?

As if I were part of their chorus, I said, "I do forgive you though."

I have never seen anyone's face change so fast. It was like hope turned on a light inside her head.

"That doesn't mean I'm ready to come back and live with you though," I said quickly. "I'm really happy where I am. I have a good life now."

She closed her eyes for a second, like somebody trying to regain her balance. When she opened them, the tears were gone.

"It's going to be a long, long time before I'm ready to even suggest that," she said. "I'm just learning how to cope with myself. It would be criminal for me to take you away from your home when I can't be the kind of mother you need yet. It looks like all your needs are being met."

"All my holy hungers," I said.

She looked at my chest. "Is that what your shirt says under your overalls? Something about holy hungers?"

"Yeah," I said.

"This is all I need right now," she said. "This is more than I even dared hope for."

She sat back in the seat and sighed, like she was breathing out about four years' worth of misery. I sat back, too, and my hand hit the cookie tin I'd carried in with my gratitude journal.

"Oh," I said, "speaking of hunger, I want to say my three favorite words to you."

"Your three favorite words?" she said. "Those are . . . ?"

"Have a cookie," I said. I slid the tin onto the table and pried off the lid. "I didn't totally make them myself, but I helped. Now Marissa, that's one of the Flagpole Girls, she's an incredible cook. I would have brought some of her enchi-

ladas, but I don't think they would like that here. Hey, you
want a milkshake to go with these? My treat."

I dug into my pocket and pulled out the ten-dollar bill.

"My, my," my mother said.

"I'm starting to earn some money," I said. "I make jewelry."

She nodded at my earrings. "Did you make those?"

"Sure. You want me to make you some? I won't charge
you. I mean, 'cause I know what it's like not to have any
money, or much, anyway. I don't know if you would wear
them—"

"Oh, Cheyenne," she said. "You are an angel."

We ordered milkshakes, and we talked some about how
she was painting again. That was about it. It was easier to
think of things to say when I was getting to know Ms. Race
and Norie and everybody, but I figured I could cut her some
slack. She didn't have everything we had.

We didn't even get to the gratitude journal when a woman
in a sweatshirt that said "Higher Powered" on it came over to
our table and smiled at my mother.

"Time to go?" Valerie said.

"I'm sorry," the woman said. "I hope you've had a nice
time though."

"Wonderful," she said. "Just wonderful."

She asked me if she could call me, and I said of course. I
expected to breathe this big sigh of relief when she walked
away, but I didn't. I just felt light. Nothing was pressing on my
chest or screaming in my head. I felt free, like the day I'd
walked out of the bead store after confessing. I guess the forgiveness thing makes you feel that way, no matter which side
you're on.

This time, though, we had no big celebration when we got
back to Tassie's. Oh, we ate cookies, drank hot chocolate, and
smiled a whole bunch, but it wasn't a whoopin' and hollerin'
kind of thing. I really wanted just to be quiet. Especially
when, while everybody was listening to Wyatt's version of

sitting in Denny's while I took care of my mother, Fletcher, who was sitting next to me, slid his hand along the floor until it touched mine, and then he held on to it. Then there was no reason to talk at all.

When he let go to get up and go to the bathroom, I wandered into the kitchen for a minute by myself. Weird, huh? I don't know, I was feeling so unfamiliar to myself I just needed some space. Ms. Race was in there making more hot chocolate.

"I got Tassie to lie down for a while," she said. "The poor woman is exhausted. I don't think she's slept since Avery disappeared. Did you know the police were here while you were gone?"

"No," I said. "What for?"

"They just wanted to let Tassie know they had questioned that Kenny character, and he said he never took Avery to Sacramento."

"He's such a liar," I said.

"Well, maybe, but he said he started to think about how he might get in trouble for taking a minor across the state line so he took him out to the bus station in Sparks instead."

"And just dumped him?" I said. "How come Avery hasn't come home or called or something?"

"Kenny said Avery told him that if none of you here cared enough about him to go with him, forget you all. Those weren't his exact words, of course, but he just wanted to go off on his own. He wouldn't even tell Kenny where he was going."

I sat down hard on a kitchen chair. "Is this my fault?" I said. "Did I give him the idea?"

"No, I think he was waiting for an excuse to stop trying. He didn't have enough to hold him, like you did."

"You know what I finally figured out?" I said.

"What?" she said. She turned off the burner and sat down across from me at the table.

"I figured out God really does love me. You tried to tell me, but I think I had to know it for myself."

"I think I can just lay down and die now, Cheyenne," Ms. Race said, although she looked less like an almost-dead person than anybody I knew. Her face was all bright, and her eyes were sparkling. Now, *there* was an angel.

"How will you pray now?" she said.

"Do I get to ask for things now?" I said. "You told me just to say thank you."

"Depends on what you ask for," she said. "Remember the holy hungers."

"Right."

"Just test each one. If it isn't something Jesus would want for you, don't ask."

"Actually," I said, "I don't think I'll ever ask for anything again. I already have it all!"

She reached over and squeezed my wrist. "I saw you holding hands with that cute Fletcher."

I giggled. I kept giggling when the phone rang, and she answered it.

I stopped, though, when her face started to go grim. She put her hand over the mouthpiece and said, "Go wake up Tassie."

All of Tassie's kids gathered around her in the kitchen when she took the phone from Ms. Race. She just said uh-huh a bunch of times before she hung up. Her face was gray.

"Was it about Avery?" Ellie said.

She nodded. "They found him out in Sparks. At a crack house."

"A crack house?" I said. "I thought he was going to take a bus somewhere."

"From what they could get out of him, he said Kenny took him to the crack house. There never was any bus station." She chewed hard on her lower lip. "He's been so far out of it, no wonder he didn't call."

Beside me, Brendan swore under his breath. Then he stalked out of the kitchen, and I heard him go out the front door.

"I have to go down to the police station," Tassie said.

"I'll take you, Ma," Diesel said.

"What do you want us to do?" Ellie said.

"Just take care of each other." Tassie's big chest heaved. "I don't want to lose any more of my children."

"Where's Brendan?" Ellie said when Tassie and Diesel were gone.

"He's out on the front porch," Felise said from the kitchen window.

"I better bring him in. He's so stupid, he would freeze to death and not even know it."

But Felise grunted at her. I joined Felise at the window and peered out myself, and I grinned. "Brendan's all right," I said. "He has Tobey on one side and Brianna on the other. They won't let him do anything stupid."

"You guys going to pray?" Felise said.

I looked at her in surprise. "Yeah," I said, "I guess we should."

Dude, I'd been wrong. There was always going to be something to ask for.

The next couple of weeks were so different, I had to keep looking at myself in the mirror to see if I was the same person. Even that didn't tell me much. I liked the new 'do so much I kept it, and Ellie ended up giving me the lip gloss because I borrowed it all the time.

I guess you could say Fletcher and I started "going out." Neither one of us had a car or anything, so basically we hung out together at school and went places with the whole group. Tassie had him over for dinner, but he always got really shy at the table with all of us. He wasn't that goofy once you got to know him. He was in my gratitude journal every night. At least once.

Avery never did come back to live with us. Although his

four days in the crack house were his first big-time experience with drugs, he came out of there pretty messed up. We
all went to see him in the hospital, and it was sad. He didn't
seem to recognize any of us except Brendan. Too bad. He had
walked away from his only real friend.

Now Brendan, on the other hand, turned into this whole
other person after Avery left. He quit going over to the Don't
Give a Hang gang, and instead of skateboarding every time
Tassie would let him out of the house, he started to work on
the truck with Diesel. They smelled a lot alike, but it was better than cigarette smoke.

Ellie took over Avery's job as family smart aleck, but we all
pretty much blew her off when she did that. She told me, if I
let my nails grow out, she would do them for me. I didn't
jump right on that. After all, I still had my mother to deal
with.

Valerie—Mama—and I made Saturday afternoons at
Denny's a regular thing. That was good, because if we had
gone someplace private, we might have gotten into some
pretty big fights. I had stuff I just had to get out about what
she had done to me. I found out forgiveness doesn't mean you
don't still have to work things through. No, I needed those
fingernails to chew on.

My mom did get around to asking me about the gratitude
journal. The next week she brought me a wooden cross she
had painted a dove on, and I wore it on a ribbon around my
neck. It was gorgeous. She was so gifted. I mean, the woman
had real talent.

Anyway, everything was so different, especially the feeling
I had inside. Not that I didn't still have rude thoughts sometimes—like when people got on Brianna because she was
black, which is another whole story, or when guys couldn't
keep their hands off of Marissa, which is also a whole other
thing—but the center of me, you know, where all the other
feelings come out of, that was like this peaceful pool. And
when I looked into it at night when I'd written in my journal

and I was lying there praying, I'd see myself as a whole different Cheyenne. My mother had said I was an angel. Not quite. But I thought what that lady had said to me so long ago in Winnemucca was true: I was a good person.

Things had settled down some when Valentine's Day came along, so I was feeling like this little feather-person, you know, I was so free and all. That day was one I'd been looking forward to ever since about a week before when all us Flagpole people had decided to change it to Holy Hungers Day.

As soon as the bell rang for lunch, I tore into the theater lobby with my contribution to the celebration, a plate heaped with heart-shaped cookies I'd helped Tassie bake, with Marissa and Shannon in there, too, of course.

I set them in the middle of the circle and sat down next to Fletcher, who first blew some popcorn at me with a straw, and then wove his fingers in with mine and started on a slow smile. He was so adorable—but, you know that.

The rest of the food appeared, including this humongous box of chocolates Norie's mother had bought for us. It must have cost fifty bucks. Well, that's nice.

Once we had the entire buffet spread out, Tobey said, "Let the bingeing begin!"

Some of it was on food. The rest was on telling about our holy hungers. It was better than chocolate, I mean it.

Tobey's was for every one of her relationships to be real, like hers were with all of us. Brianna's was to be seen as a person, not a black person. She said she was tired of being a color. Ms. Race, she wanted every kid at King to be a Flagpole kid. That wasn't a hunger—that was starvation!

Even the guys told about their holy hungers. Fletcher, of course, goofed around first and said his was for a Ferrari. When I smacked him, he came out with the real one. "I have this hunger to just be allowed to be me, you know?" he said. "I'm sick of being what I'm expected to be."

I squeezed his hand, and he squeezed back. That meant we were going to work on that.

When it was my turn, I said, "I had a hard time picking one."

"You can only tell one, girl," Brianna said. "We don't want to be sitting here till graduation."

"No," I said, "I mean, I couldn't pick even one, because I have everything. But then I thought, 'Y'know, everybody doesn't have everything—well, actually they do, only they don't know it. I mean, it's like we probably all have everything we need or the ability to have it, right inside us where God put it, only we don't know it or we can't get it out." I stopped for breath. Nobody was giving me the hurry-up sign. In fact, they looked kind of entranced. "So here's my point," I said. "My holy hunger is to always appreciate what I have and help other people appreciate what they have. That isn't all that deep, but—"

"Oh, that's deep, all right, girl," Brianna said. "It's so deep, I'm not sure I even understand it."

"But I love it," Tobey said. "You are so cool, Cheyenne."

"Thank you," I said.

Then I reached for the chocolates box and kept on binge-ing—on only the holiest pieces, of course.

Look for Other Books in the Raise the Flag Series
by Nancy Rue

Book One: *Don't Count on Homecoming Queen*
Tobey suspects Coach is up to something sinister at King High, and only the Flagpole Girls can help her figure out what to do!
ISBN 1-57856-032-2

Book Two: *"B" Is for Bad at Getting into Harvard*
Norie's faced with the chance of getting the grades she's worked so hard to attain, at a tremendous cost. Will she cheat or find another way?
ISBN 1-57856-033-0

Book Three: *I Only Binge on Holy Hungers*
Cheyenne only wants to fit in. Shoplifting seems to be the means to an end. It will take her Christian friends to help her find the way out.
ISBN 1-57856-034-9

Book Four: *Do I Have to Paint You a Picture?*
Brianna and the Flagpole Girls learn that keeping the peace is rough business when the rumblings of racial tension escalate into real-life violence.
ISBN 1-57856-035-7

Book Five: *Friends Don't Let Friends Date Jason*
When Marissa finds out that the first boy she's ever fallen for is a user, she learns that a healthy self-esteem is worth more than an inflated ego.
ISBN 1-57856-087-X; *Available in 1999*

Book Six: *Untitled*
Shannon's wonderful Christian family is falling apart because her sister Katelyn has gone wild. Will her parents ever see the "good kid" in Shannon hiding in the shadows?
ISBN 1-57856-088-8; *Available in 1999*

Join millions of other students in praying for your school! See You at the Pole, a global day of student prayer, is the third Wednesday of September each year. For more information, contact:

See You at the Pole
P.O. Box 60134
Fort Worth, TX 76115
24-hour SYATP Hotline: 619/592-9200
Internet: www.syatp.com
e-mail: pray@syatp.com